THE
CURSED
HUNTER

THE CURSED HUNTER

Copyright © 2019 by Bethany Atazadeh

Contact Info *: http://www.bethanyatazadeh.com*

Cover Design by : Bethany Atazadeh
Editor: Enchanted Ink
Formatting Template : Derek Murphy

Third Edition: August 2023
10 9 8 7 6 5 4 3

THE CURSED HUNTER

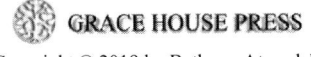

GRACE HOUSE PRESS

AHDAMON

JINN

SAGH

HODAFEZ

HUMAN
KINGDOMS

W E

S

RUSALKA

DRAGON CLIFFS

KESHDI

AZIZ

PIRUZ

BARADAAN

1

HEAVY WINGS BEAT THE hot air, almost too soft to hear unless already listening. I whirled around.

A dragon.

It was the size of a bird in the distance, but its long, arching neck and tail were unmistakable. So was its speed—it was growing fast.

I pulled back against the rocky cliffside, hiding in a cleft, heart pounding. Below me was an enormous drop. The trees and bushes were the size of my fingernail; the sliver of river that wound through the forest beyond the Dragon Cliffs was nearly invisible at this height. If I miraculously didn't smash into the rocks on the way down, the sharp tree branches would break my fall. Permanently.

I wasn't supposed to be here.

Keep your focus, Nes, I coached myself, waiting a long stretch until I could be sure the dragon was gone. A mistake on the cliffs could be deadly. They stretched on as far as the eye could see, all sharp angles, and jutting heights. Occasional patches of green grass and ragged bushes dotted the otherwise dusty landscape.

Only the toughest creatures and vegetation lived in these heights. My lips curved in a smile as I pushed higher.

Some of my hair had come loose from the braid and stuck to my skin, damp from the unforgiving sun beating down on me; I pushed the dark strands behind my ear. Besides my nearly black hair and boots, the rest of my ensemble was designed to blend in with the tan rocks, which were just a few shades lighter than my own skin.

Reaching back, I thrust my hand into the bag hanging at my hip, rubbing the white powder between my sweaty palms to dry them. The climb was nowhere near the end, even though my arms and legs shook with exhaustion.

I'd shed my coat at the base of the cliffs before beginning my ascent, but despite my loose, sleeveless shirt and lightweight climbing pants that stretched and breathed with my movements, I was sticky and overheated.

This was farther than I'd ever climbed before. I'd been pushing myself, training my body to go higher each time, returning with limp noodles for limbs. The burn in my muscles was brutal.

But also thrilling.

My quest for a dragon's egg was one that few had ever accomplished. Avizun was our town's greatest dragon hunter—he had the most kills since he'd joined the Dragon Watch in Heechi.

Not many dragons flew within range of our little town. Usually they swerved just out of reach—unless they'd gotten a taste of livestock or possibly even human flesh, and were unable to help themselves. When they did test our watch, Avizun's arrow tended to be the one that brought them down.

But most of the time, the dragons kept to the great heights and the wilderness, and us humans went to them.

Sometimes the hunters pursued the beasts instead of the eggs. Their scales, teeth, and claws were all quite in fashion. And there were those on the market for dragon meat, even if our own citizens found it disgusting. But above all else, it was their eggs that were prized. They were luminescent. More beautiful than any other creation and more durable than diamonds. Many hoped to someday find a living egg, instead of only pieces, and raise a dragon of their own in captivity. Such a thing had never been done.

Avizun had been on the hunt for a dragon's egg for the last two decades—since before I'd been born—and had only pieces of eggshells to show for it. All seven eggshell pieces he'd brought back over the years were proudly mounted in the Heechi museum and neighboring towns.

These days, he hunted with a twelve-man crew, but rumor said back when he'd hunted solo, he'd once faced a dragon and lived. Most people questioned that story, but I'd only shrugged. Dragons were intelligent—more so than some humans—and known to play with their food.

The real question that no one asked was why did the dragon survive their encounter? Perhaps it simply chose to let the great hunter go. My money was on that scenario.

I supposed the failure of a renowned dragon hunter like Avizun should've made me question if it was even possible for an eighteen-year-old girl. I grinned at the thought. The impossible was what I lived for.

Somewhere out of view, a dragon roared. Maybe the same one I'd seen before, or maybe another.

Goosebumps pebbled on my bare arms where just moments ago I'd been sweating. I'd heard the sound many times, but the experience was far more terrifying up close.

Maybe I'd climbed farther into dragon territory than I'd realized.

Still, the only way to find a dragon egg was to enter a dragon's lair. The occupation naturally came with some risks.

I allowed myself to rest another minute, until I felt certain the dragon was out of range.

Taking out my hammer and another metal stake, I pounded it into the cliff as an anchor. Though I could free-climb easily enough when I was fresh and invigorated, my strength at this point in the climb was always in question. A wise climber always used rope if possible.

Fortunately, a few years back, when my family's circumstances had been different, I'd invested in a Jinni-spelled rope that grew and tightened as needed.

A rare find, especially in our part of the world. Both pure-blooded Jinni and humans touched with a Jinni's Gift avoided the Dragon Cliffs. Humans without Gifts even more so. Only those born and raised in Heechi or the nearby villages dared to live so close to the predatory creatures.

The cool tingle of Jinni magic brushed my skin when I touched the otherwise ordinary woven hemp— a reminder of its power.

A tug on the rope and it stretched, letting me climb higher; a squeeze to contract when I climbed down at the end of the day. It could take me across the entire mountain range if I wanted it to.

Once the stake was firmly hammered into the rock wall, I threaded the rope through the sturdy metal loop at the top to secure myself to this new checkpoint. The checkpoints were a pain, but without a spotter, they were a necessary pain.

I rolled my eyes as I began to climb once more. My family thought I was crazy. The whole town thought I was insane.

Just this morning, as I'd walked through town, the children ran through the streets after me, yelling, "What's the egg girl found lately?"

I'd ignored them until they returned to their games.

A mother haggling over fish shook her head as I passed through the marketplace, nudging the vendor so he could shake his head at me too.

I'd kept my chin high.

I passed by a small group of hunters clustered around the swordsmith and his newest creation. "Haven't found anything yet, hmm?" It was the condescending tone of one of the hunters, who'd spotted me coming.

The man next to him did a poor job of hiding his smile. "You're our good luck charm," he said, elbowing Avizun, their leader.

"Our rabbit's foot," Avizun answered with a wink in my direction. "Don't stop. We need the dragons to watch for the egg girl while the real huntsmen search."

A twinge that I couldn't ignore made me scowl at them and throw up a crude gesture.

Who cares what they think? I'll show them.

They only cackled louder.

I was tall for a girl, taller than some of them; I lifted my chin, staring down my nose at them, and tried not to notice.

Even my siblings had picked it up in the last few years.

"Do you have to constantly pretend to be a hunter?" Shadi had whined as I'd left the house. "Couldn't you dress fashionably for once? I'm tired of being related to the egg girl."

Only my father called me by my given name. "Nesrin," he would say, "your mother and I are concerned."

Whether they were worried about me or their reputation, I was never entirely sure.

Still, I was determined.

I slammed another stake into the cliff, taking out my frustration on the sand-colored rock. The wind died down, until there was utter silence, besides my heavy breathing. I paused to rest. Without the focus of finding the next handhold, my mind drifted back to earlier this morning once more.

I'd strode toward the edge of town, pretending not to hear their loud whispers. Maadar Bozorgi had reached out a wrinkled hand to stop me as I passed.

"Don't worry about what people say, *dokhtari*."

The affectionate title made the corner of my mouth twitch, and I let her delay my journey out of respect. Most people thought Bozorgi was crazy.

"You have the spirit of the *Khaanevaade*." That. That was why they thought she was crazy. The Khaanevaade were a fable even older than the Jinn. The supposed ancestors of the dragons. I resisted the urge to roll my eyes.

Her grip tightened, surprisingly strong for such an old woman.

I took a deep breath, before glancing down to meet her dark eyes, nearly black like my own, like the eyes of everyone in Heechi. "I don't care what they say, Maadar. I'm going to prove them wrong anyway."

"It's normal to care, *dokhtari*." She ignored my words completely. The wrinkles around her eyes deepened as she smiled and revealed a lack of teeth, patting my arm a few more times before she let go. "What takes the sting away is if you know who you *are*. The untruths will roll off you like water off a dragon's back."

I rolled my eyes at the memory, forcing myself to focus on the jagged rocks in front of me. A tiny edge allowed me enough room to slide along one foot at a time until I reached a narrow shaft, just big enough to squeeze inside. Within the safety of the rock, I pressed my hands and feet against both sides and shoved myself up, allowing for a brief free climb until it opened out onto a wide ledge, where I stopped to catch my breath.

Maadar Bozorgi was exactly as crazy as everyone said she was.

So, maybe I was too.

Calling myself otherwise wouldn't help me; what I needed was to prove them *wrong*. The price a single dragon's egg could fetch would feed my entire family of six for a decade or more. I'd be the world's greatest dragon hunter and save my family, all in one.

I pulled my chalk bag around to powder my hands again before standing to continue my climb. My father tried to take care of us, but he'd experienced round after round of ill luck. The worst of which had taken place just last month: The Shah's Council had ruled that grain should be made available to all the people at no cost, purchased by the crowns at a fixed price. A low price. Suddenly, my father's largest crop, the one we depended on most, was reduced to the price of dirt.

I pushed upward with my legs to give my sore arms a break. My knee scraped the cliffside and ripped a hole in my soft pants, but I barely noticed.

We should be wealthy. I gritted my teeth at the thought. We worked hard enough, and my father had saved every scrap over the years so that, even with four children, we'd be okay. But the Shah's Council ruined everything. Heechi and the nearby towns would be better off on their own.

Up ahead and to the right, I spied a large cleft in the rock wall. From this angle, it was impossible to tell how large it was. Could a dragon fit there?

Only one way to tell.

I paused to reach back and pound in another stake, but I'd run out. I should've bought more before I left. Running my tongue along my teeth, I thought through my options and decided to press on. Soon, I was close enough to peer inside the crevice. It yawned wide before me, large enough for a horse, perhaps deep enough for a small wagon, but too small for a full-grown dragon. A female would need twice this space to stretch their wings, and a male three or four times as much.

Disappointed, I rested my face on the rock wall for a moment and closed my eyes.

A shrieking wind blew past and the air grew hot.

I scrambled away from the opening, almost slipping in my haste, squeezing on the Jinni-spelled rope and burning my hands as I went. I cursed myself for climbing too far and allowing myself to be distracted.

Seconds later, a roar heated the air to such a level that sweat dripped down my back. I flinched at the proximity. That couldn't have been more than a stone's throw away. I froze on the wall like a wild hare exposed on an open plateau with nowhere to go. Maybe the beast wouldn't see me.

The logic was flawed. Not logic at all really, but instinct. I let another second pass and convinced myself it'd flown by and this was my chance to climb down before it came back.

With no way of knowing if that was true, I scrambled down the cliffside until I reached the small shelf where I'd rested last. Everything in me wanted to huddle against the tiny indent in the rock wall, shut my eyes, and pray.

Instead, I fumbled with the knots, pulling my Jinni-rope free and leaving the stake behind.

One step after the other, a foothold here, a handhold there, I lowered myself with practiced speed, but still felt like I was crawling.

Heat spread across my back.

Different from my sweat, which now soaked the back of my shirt.

It was like a warm breath from a furnace.

Or a dragon.

2

A SHIVER RUSHED OVER me as I whirled around.

An enormous black dragon flew toward me on silent wings. If his size wasn't enough indication, the horns by his ears confirmed he was a male. He'd closed the distance so fast that I could see the catlike irises of his yellow-gold eyes. He reared back, revealing flames that burned in his throat, glowing red-hot.

Throwing myself against the wall, eyes squeezed shut, I cringed. In stories, they always said your life would flash before you, but all I could think was one word: *Stupid. Stupid. Stupid.*

I never should've come here.

I knew better.

Will I feel the fire before it turns me to ash?

Nothing happened.

Daring to open my eyes, I peeked behind me again. The beast flew in a lazy circle above me, taking his time. He was larger than the biggest draft horse back home—five times their size if I counted his vast wingspan.

In one heartbeat, I took in his impenetrable black scales, talons the size of my head, and the graceful curve of his wings. Awe or fear, or maybe both, made me want to throw up.

His eyes were locked on mine.

This was it. I was about to become charred flesh. Good thing I'd used stakes—that would help them find my remains tied to the cliff. Then again, maybe the dragon wouldn't leave anything behind…

For some reason, he didn't immediately attack.

Don't question a Jinni's Gift, just take it, I repeated the old saying as I scrambled away from him.

A foothold that I normally would've tested broke beneath me and I fell without either hand on the rope tied to my harness. In the precious time it took to reach down and squeeze the Jinni-rope to tighten, I fell at least a dozen paces.

The rope responded to my squeeze, jerking my fall short. The harness around my hips and waist dug into my skin like a knife. I slammed into the cliff wall. With the air knocked out of me, I hung suspended and gasping, trying to get my breath back.

Above me, the dragon's wings still flapped as his circles grew increasingly smaller. His eyes were mesmerizing. Unlike the stuffed dragon in Avizun's home, with shiny glass bulbs in the eye sockets, this dragon's eyes were so expressive I almost expected him to open his mouth and speak to me.

I shook myself, breaking the spell. Taking the rope in both hands, I yanked myself across the rock wall with almost Jinni-heightened strength, adrenaline pumping, using any crack or the tiniest of shelves for leverage.

The dragon continued to roar, soaring past me from one side to the other, watching intently. He was playing with his food.

Frustrated, I reached the small shelf and freed my hands just long enough to reach deep into my bag. The tiny bottle of pepper juice was for an unwanted suitor, but I was desperate. Uncorking the jar, I flung it at the dragon as he passed by once more.

If I'd thought his roars were loud before, this one eclipsed them all, shredding my eardrums as he dropped back in a free fall, clawing at his eyes and nose. He caught himself quickly enough. I should've known he didn't need to see to fly, but it bought me time.

Unhooking my rope, I raced down the cliff wall, scrabbling and slipping. The sharp rocks ripped at my skin and clothing, but in the panic, I didn't even feel it.

I reached the next checkpoint, and the next, before he shot past me in a blur.

His huge body crashed into the rock wall, making it shake and sending more shards of rock bouncing down the cliffside toward me. I couldn't tell if he was trying to land or shake me off. He surprised me by launching himself off the wall and flying away from the cliffs at top speed.

I swallowed and worked faster, fumbling in my haste. Was he getting ready to charge? I'd seen it on occasion when the Dragon Watch's perimeter was tested by an inquisitive dragon. Those charges were always accompanied by a furious blaze that had once or twice caught the Watch by surprise and burned a few homes before they stamped it out.

However, this dragon wasn't roaring, breathing fire, or showing any displays of dominance or aggression. I was at a loss.

While we knew a good number of facts about dragons, being that Heechi was by far the closest town to the Dragon Cliffs, most of our facts were about dragons that were either dead or about-to-be-dead.

If a human learned more intimate details about a living dragon, that human was unlikely to live long enough to tell anyone.

Shaking, I pushed myself to keep going.

In my terror, I made multiple mistakes, choosing handholds that slipped out from under me.

More than once, I didn't catch myself in time.

The rope always caught my fall, slamming me back into the cliffs over and over.

My ribs screamed in protest.

It effectively moved me down the mountain faster than ever before.

I reached another checkpoint, and another.

The dragon didn't return. Only blue skies with soft wisps of clouds surrounded me.

By the time my feet touched the leafy forest floor, I was a quivering mess. All the pent-up terror washed over me and I curled up on the grass and dirt beneath the trees and sucked in deep breaths until my ears stopped ringing.

Though no one had seen, I shook myself. *Enough weakness.* I pulled myself up on trembling legs, mentally preparing for the long walk home. It'd be dark by the time I got there. But that was good. Enough time to think up a story for why my entire body was covered in scrapes and bruises.

Despite taking the back roads through town, I had the misfortune of running directly into Avizun and his men. They stood clustered outside a home, preparing for a night raid on the lower cliffs while the dragons slept.

Though I stuck to the shadows, they were quick to spot me. It was hard to make out much through the jeering and whistles. *Cursed not to find anything. Should we ask where* not *to go?*

Limping past them, I held my head high and hoped the darkness hid the flush in my cheeks as one phrase slipped out above the rest. *Our little cursed hunter.*

3

I LAY IN BED for three days straight. When I first came home, my family took one look at me and sent me to my room. We couldn't afford a doctor, but my mother fetched one anyway. Apparently, I'd bruised a few ribs. I wasn't supposed to do anything strenuous for a few days, and I definitely wasn't supposed to climb.

After my close call, I didn't *want* to keep climbing. No one knew about the dragon. I'd told them I was only climbing for the joy of it when my stake slipped, that the fall was a result of my carelessness. Technically true.

Maybe it's time to give up my quest.

My mother certainly thought so. She'd scolded me soundly, then cried that I didn't love her if I continued to go out risking my life like one of the hunters, then went back to scolding. "What if you never recover?" she'd wailed. "Who will want to marry you then?"

I reminded her that my wounds healed quickly.

That only resulted in another round of scolding and forbidding me to climb again. As if that had ever stopped me before.

I sighed and stared at the ceiling and the flower paintings that hung on my bedroom walls. Old and faded, they were a reminder of former days when we'd had money to burn.

Now, the house sat still and quiet.

It was midmorning, judging by the way the sun shone in the window. My siblings were probably out. They preferred to visit their friends and avoid entertaining at home. Even if my father would allow it, they'd be far too embarrassed to let their friends know how far we'd fallen.

"What kind of noble family doesn't own proper silverware?" Zareen had said in horror last week when our father sold the good set quietly.

"Don't worry," Roohstam had told her, "When you find a rich husband, we'll buy it back." I think he'd believed it too.

Shadi burst into my room and jumped onto my mattress, making me wince. "Why are you still in bed? Get dressed and come join us in the sitting room. We're trying some new ideas." Her dark hair was done up in braids as if she or one of my sisters had spent the entire morning on it. The red tint was new. She'd taken to using an expensive dye that she often said I should use too, to fix up my "boring" hair, even though it was so dark that the red would likely be invisible.

"Nessie," she chastised me when I didn't move immediately. "The Summer's Eve Feast is in two days! We have to get ready!"

Another feast. Just the thought of it made me tired. "Maybe we should skip this one," I suggested. We couldn't afford to buy lavish gowns and still bring the required contribution to the Shah. "What did Baba say?"

"He'll come around," Shadi said with a wink. "He always does."

A heavy knock sounded at the front door of the main house, muffled by the walls, but still clear from where we were on the second floor.

"Oh no." Shadi paled. "I hope Roohstam didn't invite one of his friends here. Doesn't he know better?" She whirled out of the room before I could reply.

Curiosity got the better of me. Throwing a threadbare robe over my nightshift, I made my way down the hallway, wincing with each breath, until I could see the door from the top of the stairs. Roohstam, Shadi, and Zareen were already there, pressed against the walls and peering out.

Two burly men had entered. Father implored them to come to the sitting room for some tea.

"Please—" Something in his tone made my skin prickle with anxiety. "Let's talk in private. I'm sure we can work something out."

They'd come to our home before. A show of strength and intimidation. But today there was a squint to their eyes, an extra layer of hardness. Something was wrong. This was not a normal visit to remind us of our debts.

"Tell your master that I only need another month." My father managed to smile at them. "Two, at most. I'm leaving tomorrow morning on a trip to—"

"We've not been sent for excuses, old man," one of the men interrupted with his fist.

The crack of it hitting my father's jaw made me cry out. "No! Stop!" I moved toward the stairs, but Roohstam and Shadi held me back. The strength from my climbs and my panic allowed me to drag them down two steps before my little sister Zareen joined them, wrapping her arms around my waist.

Struggling, I could only watch as they pummeled my father. Jabs to his side and face, knocking him to his knees.

"Stop, please!" I screamed.

My mother tried to pull them off, but they shoved her back. She ran to the kitchens screaming for the cook.

The men ignored us, making sure my father's face was a mixture of smeared blood and deep, purpling bruises before they threw a piece of paper down on his still form. "You have a month," one growled, "or we'll be back."

The door clicked shut with a deceptive gentleness.

The grip on my arms loosened.

I wrenched myself away from my siblings, hurtling down the stairs and ignoring the stabs of pain in my ribs. "Baba! Baba, wake up!" I shrieked, reaching him before anyone else.

My mother reappeared in the doorway with the cook and a large kettle, holding it like a weapon and ready to swing. At the sight of my father alone on the ground, she deflated and the kettle lowered. She joined me beside him.

My siblings didn't move from their hiding place on the staircase, frozen in horror.

I didn't dare touch my father at first, for fear I'd make the damage worse. Blood gushed from his nose and a cut on his forehead. He groaned as he came to, and I felt fleeting relief.

Clutching the paper to his chest, he stared at me through bleary eyes, then at my mother and siblings. "I'm sorry you all had to see that."

I shook my head, unable to find words.

He took a few more shallow breaths and I dropped to my knees beside him, carefully taking his hand. "Baba, what happened?" I whispered finally. "Should we call for the Shah's guard?"

"No, no," he protested, coughing in agitation. "No guards. If someone could please help me to bed…"

I called the cook, the only servant we had left, to help Roohstam carry Baba to his bed.

This time when my mother sent for the doctor, he didn't come. She refused to show us the note, only muttering something about how he hadn't been paid last time.

"It's just a headache and a few bruises," Baba reassured her. "They'll heal up quickly."

Furious at the men who'd done this to him, I cleaned my father's wounds with a wet cloth, holding the fabric to the cut on his forehead when it wouldn't stop bleeding. He never complained.

"This isn't—" My mother cupped a hand over her mouth, tears welling in her eyes as she paced. "I can't…" She left the room.

"Baba," I said, now that we were alone. He'd always trusted me. "Tell me what happened. Why did those men do this to you?"

His eyes were closed, but I knew he was still awake from the way they fluttered and his fingers occasionally twitched.

Instead of answering, Baba clutched the paper tighter before loosening his grip and holding it out to me.

Carefully, I unrolled the parchment and smoothed out the wrinkles. I gasped at the numbers written there in careful ink. "What's this?" I whispered, "Is this what we owe them?"

"I only wanted to take out a loan for a short time." My father wheezed, as if deep breaths were impossible. "I never meant for it to go unpaid. This is my fault."

I made him chew on a few leaves of the *kushta* plant to dull the pain, arranging the blankets and pillows in an effort to help him feel better. "It'll be okay, Baba. Don't worry." I injected false hope into my voice as I dug some thread out of my mother's sewing kit.

I pulled open the curtains a bit wider, letting them shine light on the mostly empty room, revealing patches along the wall and floor where furniture, mirrors, and paintings used to be.

My father winced at the light, but I would need it to sew the nasty cut on his forehead shut.

At first, I thought the medicine might make him fall asleep, but he shook his head, almost imperceptibly, and whispered, "I'm afraid I don't know what to do."

I was shaken. My father never said things like that. He always had his optimism. Quietly, I began to sew his skin back together, wincing with him at each tug, until a crooked row of *x*'s lined his brow.

By the time I'd cleaned the wound once more and put away the supplies, his soft snores filled the room. I lifted the parchment off the table, careful not to let it crinkle, taking it with me as I slipped out.

4

THE CREDITORS' NOTE SHOOK in my hand as I read it in full, standing in the empty back stairwell. My father had exactly one month to come up with the sum he'd borrowed—plus interest—or they'd begin to extract payment. First, they would take our home. And when that didn't cover our debt, my siblings and I would be next.

I slipped back into my father's room to replace the parchment, wincing at the sobs coming from my mother's adjoining rooms.

My siblings' footsteps overhead were subdued. They'd each visited my father, one at a time, and he'd assured them they should continue on with their day's festivities and not worry about him.

I couldn't imagine wasting time on such frivolous things right now, and instead made my way out to the inner courtyard, to sit by the pool. In the shade of the pomegranate trees, I dipped my toes in the shallow water and stared at the lily pads.

By evening, I had a plan.

While my siblings drank away their worries, and my mother wept, I got to work. There was no time to lose.

Packing took little time. I'd ventured into the woods on my own more times than I could count. My father had given up trying to explain to me what girls did and didn't do long ago, after admitting I could take care of myself as well as any son. Better than most sons, actually, which I think he secretly took pride in.

I packed climbing rope and all the stakes I owned. I'd need to purchase more on my way out of town. A small hammer for the stakes went in next, followed by a hunting knife, a coat for chilly nights, and blankets for a makeshift tent. All went in my favorite bag.

I considered my flint for a fire, but decided to leave it. A fire would only be a beacon to the dragons.

By the time I finished, it was dusk. I doubted anyone would notice if I snuck out right then and there. Still, it'd be better to start in the morning, to have a full day ahead.

With that decided, there was nothing to do but wait. I crawled into bed to rest my aching ribs, but I couldn't sleep.

When my siblings came home, giggling through the halls, I listened until the big house settled into quiet creaks and silence. Only then did I creep down to the kitchen to fill my canteen to the brim with well water.

I packed venison, cut and dried in strips, along with bread, nuts, and fruit, enough for a few days at least.

Back in my bedroom, I added these to my pack in the light of the moon before stashing it under the bed. Now I just needed a good night's rest to prepare for what I would need to do tomorrow.

But as the sun rose, touching my face gently, I found my father still intended to follow through with his own plan.

"Nesrin," my father called from downstairs just as I was trying to decide the best way to slip out, his voice muffled through my closed door. He yelled for my siblings, as well as my mother, calling everyone to come.

He shouldn't be out of bed.

I shoved my bag back under the bed, rushing downstairs.

I found him in the inner courtyard, standing in the sun. "What is it, Baba?" I asked, out of breath, reaching him first.

My ribs barely ached anymore, but he hadn't had nearly as much time to recover. He winced as he sat on the closest bench, leaning against the elegant swirls in the wood and sighing in relief.

"Come, sit by me," was all he would say, giving me a pained smile.

One by one my siblings wandered into the courtyard, annoyed at the interruption. "I need to get ready, Baba," Shadi whined.

"Shadi," I snapped, but my father held up his hand and just smiled at his eldest daughter.

My mother's heels clicked down the hallway, and when she appeared in the arch, he finally began. "I've decided to keep my plans to go on my business trip. It's even more important now that I don't delay. If all goes well, it should provide enough to cover our debt—"

"Shh, darling," my mother interrupted, "the children don't need to be bothered with such things." Her eyes were red rimmed from weeping.

"Why? Is it a secret?" I challenged, turning from her to my father, taking his hands in mine. "Baba, is this trip really going to cover the debt?"

"Don't worry about me, little dragon hunter." His smile crinkled the corners of his eyes and stretched his white beard. I hated the nickname, hated the way he used it to tease me, just like the townspeople. "Tell me, what would you all like me to bring back for you?"

I could only blink at him.

It was an old tradition he'd begun when we were little *bache*. Each business trip, he'd ask what we wanted and bring back a trinket for each of us, no matter how extravagant.

"Ooh, can I have one of those jade hair pins?" Shadi stepped forward, gesturing to her red hair. "They would accent my coloring perfectly."

"Jade hair pins," my father repeated, lowering his spectacles to the tip of his nose, pretending to write it on an invisible list.

"A sword for me, Baba," Roohstam jumped in. "The kind that are half the length of a regular sword— they're extremely high fashion."

A knock sounded at the door. "Could you get that, Maadar?" he asked my mother absently.

My father turned to his youngest. "Zareen?" He nodded through her list of ideas, as if they were nothing.

"And for you, Nesrin?" he said finally, turning to me where I'd sat silently fuming.

"I don't need anything, Baba."

"Oh, come now." His forehead wrinkled as if the thought of *not* spending money on me caused him distress.

I pondered climbing equipment or a new bag for my chalk dust that kept my hands dry, but I couldn't bear to ask for anything. My throat swelled shut.

"Are you going far?" I managed to ask.

Frowning a little, my father nodded. "Across the kingdoms."

"Then bring me a flower from this other land. Something we don't have here."

His eyes crinkled as he smiled and shook his head at me, but he didn't argue.

My mother cleared her throat loudly. When we turned, her face was pale. Beside her stood a tall, raven-haired man with pale skin and piercing green eyes. In his presence, my skin tingled as if a breeze touched it, though the air was as dry and lifeless as a bone. No—not a man. I held my breath at the whiff of magic, as if it might infect me. A Jinni.

"This is Joram." My father gestured to the Jinni, who stared down his long nose at us. Leaning on his knees and groaning as he stood, Baba added, "I hired him last month to help me make the journey to the Shah's Council."

This time, my mother was too intimidated by the Jinni beside her to shush my father.

"Why are you still going?" Roohstam asked before I could, arching a brow.

"You all know my brilliant proposal to bring before them." Baba's voice lowered to a whisper, as if

33

the Jinni beside him wouldn't hear it. "A way to bring back the value of our crops with Jinni magic." He clapped his hands in excitement as his voice returned to normal. "It's more important now than ever that I go. I must convince them to give me a loan to cover this project, as well as our debts. I'm certain we'll make our money back tenfold before the creditors return."

"When will you be back?" My voice was flat.

"With Joram's ability to travel in an instant, we'll arrive immediately. At that point, I'll explain the details to him so he can demonstrate for the council. I assume we'll be back in just a day or two—as soon as they sign the papers."

As usual, my father's confidence had everyone grinning, shoulders relaxed, hugging him goodbye and telling him how they always knew he would find a way.

I hugged him last, not saying a word. The Shah's Council was unpredictable. Maybe the Jinni's presence would sway them. Or maybe they'd refuse to deal with Jinni magic. It was hard to say, but it certainly didn't seem like a guaranteed solution to me. I stepped back, throat closing. When Baba got an idea like this in his head, there was no arguing with him.

The Jinni stepped forward, settling a hand on my father's shoulder. A flash of magic that made my skin tingle left a space where they'd stood.

I turned to go to my rooms without a word.

He could try to save our family with this trip. I wanted to believe it would be successful. But this wasn't his first grand attempt, and I wasn't as naïve as I used to be.

To truly make sure my family and I would be safe, I needed to make a trip of my own.

* * *

I LEFT AN HOUR after my father. As far as my family knew, this was just another climb, no different from any other day.

"You should rest another week," my mother complained, eyes on her plants, pulling weeds from the dirt. She'd taken to keeping up the courtyard and other landscaping after the gardener was let go. She knew better than to try forbidding me from climbing again, but she wouldn't meet my eyes.

"I'll be fine," I assured her, stretching to prove it. It was true. The swelling had gone down and my sides barely hurt anymore.

She wouldn't even look up.

"Could you take the back roads out of town, at least?" Zareen asked from where she lounged in the shade with a foot in the pool. "People make fun of you enough as it is."

"Obviously," I muttered, turning to go.

"Need a climbing partner?" Roohstam asked as he entered the courtyard from the other side.

The corner of my mouth lifted, but I shook my head. "Not today."

"Here." Zareen stood and picked two peaches from the tree, coming over to add them to the bag on my back. "You need something to eat. Or I suppose you can throw them at people when they make fun of you." She rolled her eyes dramatically as Roohstam laughed.

Impulsively, I hugged her.

She shrugged out of my embrace with an embarrassed laugh. "I still think you should take the side roads."

"I know." I smiled at her.

One more glance around the courtyard at my family, or at least most of them—Shadi was probably napping at this hour—and then I entered the cool of the house, heading toward the front door.

They'd get my note later.

I'd left it on my father's desk to explain I'd be gone longer than normal, but not to worry. And I'd made sure to tell them that I loved them all. Just in case.

I caught myself.

I shouldn't think like that. As if I was already dead to them. There was a chance I'd survive.

A very small chance.

Oddly enough, the thought of almost certain death didn't bother me much.

My skin tingled, as if the anxiety and worry was on the outside of me, while on the inside adrenaline and excitement lit me on fire.

My father would say I had an adventurer's spirit. There was something about risk that propelled me forward instead of pushing me away.

"Danger should be your middle name," my mother used to say when I'd come home with scrapes and cuts from my explorations.

"Why isn't it?" I'd ask, and she'd roll her eyes.

"I didn't expect my daughter would be a little dragon hunter," she'd say back.

She'd stopped saying that when I first began climbing the Dragon Cliffs at fifteen. Three years later and she refused to talk about dragons at all anymore.

The Dragon Cliffs were where I headed now. It took me all morning to buy supplies and hike through the forest to where I'd climbed last. There was no sign of my fall, besides a few loose pebbles, but the spot was etched in my mind and I hurried to pass it.

Making my way along the dusty orange rock, I followed the jagged outline of the cliffs all afternoon and into the evening, until the sun was in my eyes.

Cautiously, I shaded them and searched the sky. No dark shapes hovered in the wide-open blue space filled with soft wisps of clouds; still, I kept to the forest for cover. Dragon eyesight was better than a hawk's.

And once more, I was deep within their territory.

5

NO MORE SEARCHING THE outskirts of the Dragon Cliffs. The outlying lairs might've been safer, with dragons few and far between, but the likelihood of finding an egg was almost nonexistent. I needed to not just climb the nearest heights, but move inward, over the initial cliffs, into true dragon territory.

I laid out my overnight supplies, setting up a simple canopy-style tent and laying branches over it in a careful design until it was thoroughly disguised from above. Twice I ducked under cover of the trees when a dragon flew past. The first was a shade of gold so vivid it was impossible to miss, but the second was a gray that blended into the sky, and it was nearly upon me, close enough to make out his light gray underbelly, before I hid. Dinner was cold, since a fire in this region was too risky, but it was filling.

In the morning, I'd climb where even the greatest hunters didn't go. To pass the time I counted my stakes. I'd brought twice as many as any previous climb. They would weigh me down, but I'd need them to reach new heights. Besides my Jinni-spelled rope, I had three regular ropes as backups, although if all went well, I'd never need them.

Dusk fell. I flinched when a dragon roared as it returned from hunting. More joined in until the air rumbled with a thunderous chaos that had my heart beating heavily.

Throughout the night, they called to each other. The snarls ripped through my dreams. More than once I woke in a cold sweat at the vicious sound of teeth snapping and crunching.

By morning, my eyes were puffy and swollen from exhaustion, but I stayed where I was, munching on cold jerky for breakfast as I listened to them fly off in packs or alone, to hunt or stretch their wings or terrorize a nearby village. Roars faded into the distance. I didn't dare peek out until it'd been silent for long enough to count all the individual rocks at my feet.

Finally, I stretched and packed my supplies carefully, except for my tent, which I left in place. If I survived, I'd need it when I came back down, and there was no use for it on the cliffs.

* * *

ALL MORNING, I CLIMBED. My hands paused as if they had a mind of their own whenever rocks tumbled down the cliffs or a bird cried.

As the heat of the day beat down on me, the tremor in my arms and legs changed from fear to fatigue. While much of the climb led me sideways, or sometimes back down, there were sections of the cliffs that were entirely vertical and challenged my endurance. When I found a small crevice, barely larger than I was tall and only a foot deep, I stopped to rest for a bit.

Glancing down, I was disappointed in my efforts. Normally, I'd be much farther, but with my sore ribs giving me trouble, I was slowing down already.

After eating a simple meal, guzzling some water, and catching my breath, I repacked my bag and tied it back on, returning to the cliff wall.

Another hour of climbing without a dragon in sight had eased my fears to the point that I almost screamed in terror when my eyes lifted above a rocky ledge and landed on the dusty green scales of a dragon. Its long tail stretched out toward me.

I choked on my own spit.

Coughing, I cursed myself for alerting the animal and being the cause of my own death, but the creature didn't move, didn't even shift.

Risking a closer look, my jaw dropped, and I laughed softly.

It was just the skin.

One of the beasts had shed a layer of scales like a snake. It was perfectly intact—like a second skin, minus the wings—with all the scales still linked together.

Climbing onto the small plateau, I studied the ghost of a dragon, curious. I reached out to touch it. The scales were surprisingly soft and warm to the touch from spending the morning in the sun.

Knowing I was wasting precious time, I moved closer, running my fingers along the scaly skin, and tried to rip it. It stayed smooth and strong. Taking my knife out of my bag, I tried to cut a tiny piece. When nothing happened, I stabbed the scales as hard as I could. They only dipped in from the blow, making the whole skin sag and billow before returning to its original form, undamaged. If anything, my knife seemed slightly bent.

I shook my head in awe. It would make incredible armor.

On instinct, I moved to where the dragon had first begun to scratch off the old layer, where the edges were ragged. Even here, sawing away at it with all my strength, I barely cut deeper than my little finger.

Thoughtfully, I flipped the scaly skin over, trying to remember how the artisans worked with this ridiculously tough material. It was a craft I'd never bothered to learn.

The inside of the skin was also green, but faded. I tested my knife against this side, following the lines of the scales.

It was by no means buttery smooth, but along the inside, as long as I worked with the lines between the scales, my knife made some headway. It was like cutting into a steak that had been overcooked. Or like cutting hides back home; something I'd tried once—to my mother's horror.

With this success, I spent the better part of an hour carving into the skin. It took quite a few glances to the sky and almost as many blisters before I'd finally created a poorly designed, lopsided vest that reached to my knees. There were holes for my arms, which remained bare, and smaller holes punched into the sides so I could tie the whole ensemble together using a short piece of rope.

It pained me to leave the valuable skin behind. But even if I wasted an entire day cutting and folding, there wasn't room in my bag for both the skin and an egg. And an egg was priceless.

Still.

I circled the skin, grabbing the side of it awkwardly, and began to push. It was like lifting an enormous, heavy blanket.

Struggling with the way it folded in on itself and didn't cooperate, I finally shoved it over the edge. I winced as it scraped against boulders and fell into the trees below.

It might be a challenge to get it from there, and there was no guarantee another hunter wouldn't come along and snatch it, but if I climbed down the mountains empty-handed, at least I'd have something.

Dusting off my hands, I returned to my climb. The few times a dragon returned to the cliffs throughout the day, they roared their arrival, giving me plenty of warning. Hiding was more a nuisance than anything.

No doubt, I looked foolish, but I was proud of my foul-smelling, green outfit. Not only was I more protected—as much as one could be from a beast that could breathe fire—but now I smelled like them too. The smoky stench clung to the scales the same way clothing smelled after standing beside a large bonfire for hours. The scales would help cloak my human scent.

At least, that's what I told myself as I struggled to climb in them. I wished I'd cut the scaly vest to my waist instead of to my knees, as it kept getting in the way, despite being wonderfully flexible.

The rest of the afternoon passed without incident. I was thankful I'd pushed myself during the last few months of strenuous climbing. My muscles complained, but held out.

As the sun began to set, I heard a roar and barely managed to tuck into a crevice and out of sight before a sleek, blue dragon tore past above me. It shouldn't spy my rope and stakes, which were the same color as the rock and nearly invisible unless the eye was searching for them.

The crevice I stood in wouldn't allow me to sit, much less lie down. As much as I wanted to stay here, I couldn't. But only a short climb farther was a shallow cave where I could spend the night… as long as it was uninhabited.

I swallowed at the thought.

Fingers shaking, I forced myself to keep going. In my hurry, I knocked a few pebbles loose and winced, listening to them knock against the mountainside all the way down. After holding my breath for a long moment, I rushed on, scrabbling to find purchase for my fingers and toes, pushing myself to move faster.

When I got halfway there, I had to pound in another stake. Flinching as each blow rang out, I tested it quickly and scurried up the wall, ignoring the sweat dripping down my back. I nearly kissed the floor of the small cave when I finally reached it.

Before I tied off my ropes, I scanned the darkness of the dusty sandstone alcove. Empty, besides a few stray rocks. It was barely larger than my closet back home. Satisfied, I pulled off my harness and the rope, holding in a moan as my sore muscles complained. I used a heavy rock to secure the harness and studied the skies as I stretched.

I'd made it a full day.

Carefully setting my bag on the cave floor, I leaned against the back wall. The sunset cast dancing shadows and bright orange light on the walls. A soft sigh of relief escaped my lips. I'd found a safe place to sleep.

Just in time, too.

The roars of returning dragons picked up, creating a terrifying song, just like the night before. This time, much closer.

I held my breath for long intervals. *What if they smell me?* Tucking myself deeper inside the vest of scales, I pulled it around my whole body and burrowed as far into the back of the cave as possible, shivering. Not because the air was cold—it was a warm night, even at these heights—but from the nearness of the beasts.

Sleep was fitful. If I'd thought last night was bad, the sounds were nothing compared to this.

At one point, the cliff walls shook as a fight broke out and a cascade of rocks and boulders poured down the mountainside. Was this normal?

Finally, limbs heavy with pure exhaustion, I slept.

The thunderous chorus of their morning takeoff woke me. Once it seemed safe, I began my own morning routine of breakfast and stretches, hissing at the stiffness in my sore muscles. Despite the pain, the thrill of anticipation buzzed through my veins.

I might find a dragon's egg today.

6

I STOPPED TO SEARCH every crevice. No signs of a nest or even pieces of an old eggshell.

I climbed higher.

At one point, when I glanced down, I found only a white, fluffy sea of clouds for miles in every direction. The ground was nowhere to be seen.

Though I'd spent time above clouds before, the complete lack of earth unnerved me.

On more than one occasion, the growl of a nearby dragon had me scurrying in another direction. Knowing not all the dragons flew out made me approach each new cave with extreme caution. Fortunately, they weren't nearly as quiet lumbering around on land, and I never encountered one.

My burning muscles forced me to pause more frequently as the day wore on, still tired from the day before. The air cooled and grew thin, making it harder to breathe.

I refused to let the slow progress bother me. There was still time. Still over half the day to climb, and any second now, I was certain I would discover an egg.

The cliffs stretched on endlessly on both sides. Each time I found a sizeable opening, I crept just close enough to peek inside. But always, they were empty.

Taking out my hammer, I pounded in the next stake a bit too hard. It bent sideways. I took a deep breath and blew it out, just barely able to thread the rope through. *Calm down. It's not over yet.*

Another hour passed.

I hissed as the fourth blister on my palm burst open. As much as I wanted to stop and rest, I forced myself to rub fresh powder on my hands to get rid of the sweat, ignoring the way it burned in the open sore, and kept going.

Time was running out.

By the time the sun was halfway through the sky, my optimism began to fade. That, along with my remaining soreness, made a difficult climb become grueling. *I should've found an egg by now.*

It was late spring, and many would be done hatching, but there should still be a few weeks left in the mating season. *Unless this year, they finished early?* The thought made me want to cry in frustration, but I was far too dehydrated.

Gritting my teeth, I let my irritation fuel my climb and aimed for yet another hollow in the cliff wall.

This time, once I peered inside the opening to make sure it was safe, I let myself enter and lie down, panting from exertion.

Yet again, no egg.

Despite the cooler air, sweat trickled down the side of my face. The sun burned hotter than dragon fire, or at least that's how it felt after hours spent under its unrelenting heat.

Squinting, I crawled deeper into the cave where the shade was refreshing. My eyes roved around the space and I tried to catch my breath, until a cluster of boulders in the back of the cave made me stop.

I crawled closer.

Something about the way they formed a circle almost made them look like a rough nest...

Jumping to my feet, I ran over to the strange group of rocks.

It was too good to be true. But there it was.

An egg.

It was a deep shade of aqua and speckled with white like the stars in the night sky. The old, broken shells in the town museum didn't have such rich hues. All those remnants were faded and dull.

This shell was pulsing with life.

The rock nest made the perfect hiding place. No doubt, I'd been passing eggs all day.

And yesterday.

Possibly even on previous climbs.

I half laughed and half groaned.

Leaning over, I brushed away the soft foliage and twigs over the top of the shell and my heart sank.

The small top of the egg was misleading.

It grew wider and wider as I dug it out.

The shell pieces that Avizun and the other hunters had brought back in the past were rarely larger than a hand or two.

Having never known the full size of an egg, I'd only had my imagination to go on, but I'd felt certain I could carry one.

How wrong I'd been.

This egg was nearly as tall as my waist, and while the top was deceptively small, barely larger than my fist, it was as wide as my entire arm at the bottom.

I laid my hand against the warm egg.

It's too big.

There was no way I could carry that down the mountainside. I didn't think I had the strength to lift it out of its nest.

My fingers curled into a fist against the shell.

I would *not* go home empty-handed.

My mind raced.

A resentful part of me whispered that I'd been a fool to think a dragon's egg could be carried in the first place. Sure, Avizun had found smaller pieces, but those were probably the runts. Considering the size of an adult dragon, I was willing to bet there were eggs even bigger than this one.

I needed to get moving. Before the dragons returned.

I stayed right where I was, both hands on the egg.

I was witnessing a miracle. No human had ever seen a live dragon's egg. Its warmth made me want to cradle it.

No one was watching. I let myself stroke the egg one last time and whispered, "It was lovely to meet you, little one."

Glancing outside, I regretted the lost time immediately. Dragons preferred to hunt prey during the day, but as the sun set, they would begin flying home.

Maybe I should focus on finding the remnants of a dragon's egg already hatched. And I could always climb down and find that dragon skin.

There was a tightness in my chest that wasn't from exertion, the thin air, or the heat. I kicked the huge rocks surrounding the shell. Pain shot through my toes and the boulder didn't budge.

It won't be enough.

Pieces of an eggshell would sell for a good price, but our debt was too much.

Still. *It could help.*

My lips flattened into a line and I sank down to rest on my heels, putting my head in my hands. *Maybe if I come back to search for dragon skin every few days—even a lost tooth or nail—I could piece together the full amount before the end of the month.*

I left the cave to begin my slow, tedious descent, but it was an effort to keep moving. Blisters burst on my palms. My bag was soaked with sweat where it had melded to my back. I'd come all this way for nothing.

There's still time, I reminded myself, stretching one tired foot toward a ledge, dragging my body after it.

No one else has ever found an egg before. Maybe I can find another. I thought through the options as I climbed, refusing to give up hope. *Or, maybe I can come back with a bigger bag. Maybe bring some kind of pulley system to lift the egg. Or if that doesn't work, I could hire one of the other hunters, if I can find one who won't steal the egg for his own—*

Distracted by my plans, I forgot to search for my next shelter until a roar filled the air.

Without intending to, I let out a squeak of surprise.

Peering over my shoulder, I found a black speck approaching, fast.

"Please, oh please, think I'm a dragon too," I whispered as I shimmied down the rocks, scanning the rock wall for an opening.

The closest cavity was no more than a little lip. When I reached it, it didn't hide me at all.

Just a bit farther to the side was a much larger cave. It yawned as wide and tall as the entrance to the courtyard back home.

With a quick peek at the skies, I found they were clear now. At least to my human eyes.

I'm one of you. Don't pay me any attention.

I pulled myself into the dragon-skin vest as much as possible, praying the dragon would only see the shining scales.

Ignore me, I'm one of you.

If I could make it to the cave, I could shuck the harness and the Jinni-rope and run into its depths. If it was deep enough, a dragon wouldn't be able to pursue.

Those were two giant 'ifs.'

Keeping my arms and legs pulled tight to my body, I swung into the cave, only to turn and find a black dragon flying around the side of a cliff. Closing in fast. Near enough to note, in the space of a heartbeat, that those razor-sharp claws were as big as my hand. The bared teeth even sharper.

I ripped the harness off, stumbling as I jumped out of it.

Leaving it and my Jinni-rope behind, I sprinted inside the cave.

In the shadows, bits of shell lay within a circle of boulders, but there wasn't time to cheer or snatch a piece.

I smacked into the mud and rock at the back of the cave far too soon.

It wasn't deep enough.

As I turned around and pressed into the dank wall, the dragon landed in the mouth of the cave. The tools in my bag dug into my spine.

The heavy crash made the floor shudder and a few pebbles shake loose from the ceiling.

This cave was small for the dragon. Maybe a female would've fit, but this was a large male—the horns on his head proved it.

He ducked his head and long neck, pulling in his wings until they were tucked in next to his body. His pitch-black scales glinted almost a green hue where the light touched him.

As he approached on all fours, he blocked the entrance, sucking the light out of the cave and making it feel like the sun was setting.

"Back off!" I yelled, pressing into the wall, glancing to the sides for a place to hide, but finding only smooth rock walls. "I drank a gallon of pepper juice earlier—if you eat me, you'll choke on it!"

Of all the ridiculous things to do, trying to speak to the beast was at the top of the list. Sure, they understood the human tongue—at least they seemed to, listening to our shouts during attacks on Heechi, and responding with cunning—but that didn't mean they listened.

He roared, jaws open, showing me a mouth full of curved, glistening teeth.

I squeezed my eyes shut.

A snuffling sound made me open them.

His nose twitched, smelling my makeshift armor.

I didn't dare move.

He reached out one of his long talons and prodded my side, almost like a child would poke at a strange object to see what it would do.

The gesture knocked the breath out of me.

Those strange yellow-gold cat eyes blinked and the closeness reminded me of the dragon I'd met only a few days earlier.

"You're the one who likes to play with your prey," I groaned, clenching my fists helplessly at my sides. "Just get it over with."

When I spoke, he drew back.

I cleared my throat and continued with false bravado. "Good choice. Now, get out of here before I spray you with pepper juice again."

It was back on my harness, somewhere on the cave floor behind him, but he didn't know that.

The dragon blinked once, twice. I could swear that recognition dawned in those expressive eyes.

When he roared, I flinched.

The sound reverberated in the small space.

"Are you trying to make me deaf?" I yelled back, hoping my strange behavior might scare him off.

Swallowing, I pushed off the wall and slowly inched one foot forward. Then another.

Those big, clawed feet in front of me shuffled back in response. It was working.

"You're—" I had to stop to swallow again, my mouth had grown so dry. "You're going to let me out of here. Right now, you hear me? I am *not* dying today."

Miraculously, the dragon growled and grumbled but continued to back up until his haunches reached the edge. He stopped.

I stopped too. I couldn't help it.

He was huge.

My boldness was all a show, which he might already know if he could hear my pounding heart.

I gulped, staring up at him.

The shiny black scales that lined his body and chest were the size of my head, but they grew smaller along his legs and long, snakelike neck. His long muzzle and ears reminded me of the one horse we had left in the family stables—except for those flashing fangs in his open mouth. His ears were laid back and came to a sharp point at the ends with tufts of black hair.

"Listen," I spoke over his growls, figuring I didn't have much to lose. "I need to climb down the mountain, so you need to shoo." I waved my hands at him like he was a stray.

He blinked at me and didn't move.

Sliding my foot forward, I ignored every instinct that screamed to be still, to cower back. Instead, I moved toward him, trying to stand as tall as I could and appear threatening. "Go on, shoo!"

He lifted his front feet off the rock until his head brushed the tall ceiling. I thought for a split second he might actually obey, before those big claws stretched toward me.

"No!" I yelled, turning to run, but I was too slow.

7

The Dragon

A HUMAN GIRL.

Fire surged in my belly.

KILL.

I fought the urge.

EAT.

No, that's not… that's not what I want.

What *did* I want?

I can't remember.

Red haze filled my vision. Behind it, her dark form stepped toward me. She flung her hands out.

In my throat, a snarl gripped me.

KILL. EAT. NOW.

Almost against my will, my talons stretched out. Too fast for her to react.

TAKE.

FLY.

All thought left my mind as I leapt into the air and spread my wings.

8

Nes

HIS TALONS CURLED AROUND me, squeezing tight. If not for the armored dragon skin I still wore, his claws would've pierced through me and the bag on my back.

I gasped for air as he fell backward out of the cave and his wings flew open with a whoosh.

My mouth opened in a scream that tore at my throat, but without breath in my lungs, it came out almost soundless, like a painful exhale.

I stopped struggling the moment my eyes caught on the ground, far below.

As he righted himself in the sky, wings flapping hard, we stopped free-falling and shot toward the sun instead. He carried us higher, skimming along the cliffs. Wind filled my ears and brought tears to my eyes. The ground grew impossibly small. Trees looked like toothpicks.

I wheezed, about to pass out from lack of air.

The claws loosened, almost imperceptibly.

Between the air rushing past and the blood pumping in my ears, I could hardly think.

From this angle, my main view was his black-scaled chest, so close I could reach out and touch. And just behind those scales, dragon fire.

We hurtled around the cliff walls, making my head spin. I had to close my eyes.

With a lurch that made my stomach roll over, we landed near the top of the cliffs on a huge ledge with a yawning cave mouth the size of my house. Gouged even wider by dragon talons, the space was large enough for him to keep his wings splayed.

When he dropped me on the ground, I rolled away and sprung to my feet.

Ignoring the dizziness, I took advantage of his landing, shoving off the ground to run away from him at full speed, taking in the dark cave with its pale rock walls as I went. This cave wasn't the size of my house—it was bigger.

And empty.

Nowhere to hide.

In the shadows, I nearly tripped over the uneven stone floor, but I kept running, not caring where I was going. Just *away.*

It smelled like smoke and another thick, sweet scent I couldn't quite put my finger on, so strong I could almost taste it.

Ahead, against the side of the cave, were rows of long, white bars, almost like a cage. I raced toward them with everything I had. Squeezing between the thick white bars, the straps of my bag strained against my shoulders. It wasn't until I yanked myself through and turned around, fingers brushing against the smooth sides, that I realized they were bleached bones. A shiver made the hair on my arms rise.

It *was* a cage—a dead dragon's rib cage.

Breathing hard, I spun to find the dragon prowling toward me. I backpedaled until my spine hit the opposite side of the rib cage.

His snout pressed softly against the bones.

Only a few paces between us.

Those yellow eyes blinked and he huffed. His warm, smoky breath reminded me all too well that I wasn't safe in here either.

I stood tall, staring him down. "You can't eat me if you cook me in here." My voice somehow came out strong and clear.

Avizun survived, I reminded myself, not daring to look away. *If that fool found a way, so can I.*

My hands flexed against the dragon bones at my back. Even with both hands, I couldn't circle them.

Dragon bones were nearly as impervious as their scales. *Will they protect me? Or can he break through?*

There was the possibility he'd forget about eating me and simply burn me alive.

He inhaled.

I found myself doing the same, then held my breath, waiting for death to come.

His thunderous roar filled the cave and echoed, bouncing away somewhere deep in the back of the cavern where it was too dark to see.

On and on he roared, carrying on like he was pitching a fit as he paced in front of my makeshift cage.

Despite my best efforts, I trembled a little each time he passed, waiting for the wisps of smoke to turn into fire.

One of these passes would be my last.

The adrenaline flooding through my veins wore on me. He didn't show any sign of stopping. Maybe it'd be better not to see my death coming.

With my ears ringing painfully, I sank to the ground and covered my face with my hands. For the first time since I'd left, I wished I'd told my family goodbye.

* * *

THE ROARING CUT OFF without warning. Head in my arms, my shallow breathing filled the space instead.

Pebbles rattled as the dragon lumbered around, still pacing, and then he stopped. My ears rang in the silence.

Despite my better judgment, I lifted my head and opened my eyes.

He was gone.

Leaping to my feet, I strode to the rib bones at the front and swiveled my head back and forth, searching for him. Had he flown away? With those silent wings, it was possible. More likely though, he lurked at the back of the enormous cavern in the dark, waiting for me to slip out and give him a chase.

I cursed myself for not paying attention.

As much as I wanted to run, I forced myself to wait.

And wait some more.

The smell I'd noticed underneath the smoke settled onto my skin, reminding me oddly enough of the cool tingle I always experienced when I held my Jinni-rope, or when I'd met the Jinni named Joram my father had hired for his journey.

At the thought of my father, my throat closed and I couldn't swallow. He'd declared his trip would only take a day or two, and I'd already been gone that long; he could be back from his trip by now. Or he could be trying to convince the Shah's Council at this exact moment. By the time he got home, he would learn how his daughter had been burned to a crisp on a fool's errand.

I shoved a hand through my hair and began to pace. *Focus,* I scolded myself, returning to surveying the cave. That Jinni essence was still in the air. But this was different from Jinni magic in that it wasn't just outside of me; it almost felt like a part of me. The taste of it, heavy and sweet, like a fruit I didn't recognize, sat on my tongue.

Long minutes passed as I pondered this, my eyes glued on the impossible black depths at the back of the cave. I pictured him skulking just out of sight, luring me out in false peace just so he could eat me. I waited at least another half hour, judging by the sun.

Finally, I slipped between the bones. The dragon skin I wore scraped against them on both sides. In my haste, I hadn't noticed what a tight squeeze it was, but now I was incredibly thankful I'd fit.

Approaching the front of the cave, I tiptoed slowly to the side, scanning the sky. He was nowhere to be seen. But that didn't mean he couldn't see me. If an eagle could see a mouse while circling high in the sky, a dragon could see ten times farther.

Once I'd searched every angle, I lowered my gaze to the cliffside. My Jinni-rope and harness were lost somewhere below, too far down the cliffs to see it. All I had left in my bag were my three back-up ropes. Certainly not enough to reach the ground. Especially with only a few stakes left.

Under normal circumstances, I would never free-climb, but that might be my only option.

Studying the rock walls all around, the last bit of optimism I had left disappeared. There wasn't nearly enough to hold on to for a free climb. If I attempted leaving that way, I would undoubtedly fall to my death.

Maybe if my ropes could get me to a ledge or a better climbing surface below, there was still a chance.

Not from this side of the cave mouth, though.

Risking being seen, I dashed across the opening of the cave to the opposite side, keeping an eye on the sky. The other side of the cliff was as smooth as the first. No way to free-climb down.

Especially as the sun began to set and dragons returned to their nests.

My thoughts were jumbled. I needed to sit down and eat something. Drink some water. Count my supplies and make a plan.

Before I could move, a small shape began to form in the sky, growing larger by the second. Definitely not a bird. This dragon was a female, with scales in shades of yellow and green, and from what I could tell, she was aiming for another part of the cliff. Still, I couldn't risk being seen.

I crept backward farther than seemed necessary—just in case those eyes could pierce through the darkness—and then ran to my self-imposed cage.

Only when I passed between those curved rib bones did I stop. Sinking to the rock floor, I pulled my knees against my chest and took a deep breath. I closed my eyes and just focused on that.

Inhale. Exhale.

I can find a way out of this.

Inhale. Exhale.

I'll make it home.

Inhale. Exhale.

Start by checking the supplies.

The floor quaked before me and my eyes flew open. The black dragon's impact as he landed in the mouth of the cave made the bones around me shake and clatter.

I leapt to my feet and backed up until I hit the far side of the rib cage, cursing myself when I found I was trembling again. "Get a hold of yourself!" I hissed, without taking my eyes off the beast.

He growled something almost as if in response, then resumed pacing as I stared at him.

"Just eat me already," I dared him.

I didn't know why I said it. It was rash and ridiculous.

He reared his head back and roared so loud I covered my ears. Fire shot from deep within his belly for the first time. The flames exploded down the tunnel.

Eyes wide, I pressed my lips together tightly.

Wrong thing to say.

No more talking from now on.

His fury made him bellow on and on, with little bursts of flame every so often, almost as if he couldn't help it. Thankfully, none of them were aimed at me.

I studied him as he paced. Those muscled haunches. The way his black scales gleamed in the fading sunlight, rippling like water, so smooth. Those eyes, so violent and ferocious when he first came in, were lidded and downcast as his growls died down.

With a final glance at me, he stalked down the tunnels and disappeared.

I crept to the front of my cage, peering into that sweet-smelling darkness. Cocking my head, I listened for his heavy breathing.

Nothing.

When the silence grew and the air began to cool, I frowned. *Just how deep are those tunnels? And why did he leave instead of killing me?*

Twilight loomed. Soon it'd be too dark to find a safe path down the cliffside, even if there weren't hordes of dragons approaching, roars filling the air outside. And I certainly wasn't venturing into the depths of the cave while it was occupied.

With one eye pinned to that pitch-black darkness, I tucked myself into a corner of the rib cage near the front where a large rock hid me from any approaching dragons. Kneeling, I pulled the dragon-skin armor off so I could remove my bag underneath.

I paused.

What were the odds that the dragon skin was what had stopped him? *Maybe he thinks I'm a strangely-shaped hatchling.* I shook my head almost immediately. Dragons weren't that stupid.

But the superstitious part of me quickly pulled it back on, just in case. I wouldn't allow myself to consider that wearing the skin might have been why he grabbed me in the first place.

Back in the flexible, smelly disguise, I peered into my bag in the last remaining rays of sunlight. My fingers found my canteen and I took a long sip, indulging more than I should've. Screwing the cap back on, I shook the canteen gently, listening. It was nearly empty.

Pursing my lips, I placed it carefully back inside the bag, running my fingers along the ropes I had left. I huffed in frustration.

I glanced over my shoulder frequently in case the dragon returned, but refused to let myself think about him and my impossible situation. Instead, I felt around in my bag until I found what remained of my food. A few stale pieces of bread, some jerky strips, and the remaining peach from Zareen. I didn't know how to ration the food. Should I split the supplies in half? Fourths? More than that? If I wasn't off the mountain soon, it probably wouldn't matter.

I ate the peach, a bite of bread, and a bite of jerky, then sat listening to my stomach growl and feeling sorry for myself. Another bite of bread and jerky. Enough. I stashed the rest away and pulled my bag on over the dragon-skin vest this time, just to be prepared. Every second would count if I needed to run.

Curling up on my side on the hard rock floor, I pulled my knees up to my chest for warmth and tried to sleep.

A few hours later, a soft snore filled the darkness. Startled, my eyes flew open, and for a moment I was completely disoriented. This wasn't my bedroom.

In front of me was the dark outline of a dragon in the mouth of the cave. The last few hours came crashing back. In the darkness, everything seemed grim. Impossible.

Studying the dragon through the bars of my cage, I tried and failed to discern why he'd taken me. Why he'd left me alive.

Just… *why*.

He'd returned so quietly I hadn't heard him.

Either that or I'd slept like the dead. Maybe both. I was exhausted. He may not have eaten me yet, but that didn't mean he wouldn't be hungry tomorrow.

With that thought floating around in my head, I lay there wide awake, but unable to plan. At some point, without meaning to, I finally drifted off from pure exhaustion.

✳ ✳ ✳

I WOKE TO THE ground shaking. Early morning light streamed in as the dragon lumbered past, tail swinging. When he reached the edge, he launched out into the sky and flew out of sight.

No roaring, no warning, nothing.

Just gone.

Was he waiting for me to leave the cage? How could I know if it was safe? Should I wait a few minutes, a half hour, a full hour?

I ground my teeth and kicked the bones of the rib cage. Hissing at the pain, I hopped around on one foot until it subsided.

Pulling off my bag, I tried to focus on a more immediate problem—and one I could actually solve—my growling stomach.

I took out one slice of bread and one strip of jerky, still trying to ration what I had left, and sipped at my water, which was all but gone.

Laying it out like a picnic on top of my bag, I tried to pretend it was a feast at one of those insufferable parties my siblings enjoyed so much.

"Zareen." I shook my head at my invisible youngest sister across the imaginary table. "Flattery is enjoyable, but don't you want to know what he really thinks of you? Maybe if all your suitors knew your dowry was nonexistent, you'd find out who is truly interested."

I turned toward my brother. "Stop pretending you're looking for a sword fight at dawn. One of these days you're going to get one and you know absolutely nothing about fighting."

It was so satisfying. All the things I should've said.

"Shadi." I crossed my arms and tsked at my eldest sister with her red hair dye obsession. "Red isn't your color. It makes you seem like one of the characters in the *bache's* bedtime stories."

I could imagine her gasp of outrage. A small smile crossed my lips, but it faded too quickly as I remembered this might be my last meal.

Picking up a second piece of bread, I tried to savor each bite and make it last, but just a few minutes later, I made myself stop.

Replacing the food, I pulled out the ropes next, which were all neatly wrapped. I placed them side by side on the rock floor, tying them together, one at a time, until I had one single long rope. They were lightweight material, but strong, and my knots would hold fast. That wasn't what worried me. It was the length.

I picked up my bag, holding on to the knotted rope as I slipped between the rib bones once more and crept toward the mouth of the cave.

Caution made me study the skies for a full minute before I stepped too close to the edge. Peering down the cliffside once more, I calculated how far each rope would reach until my eyes touched the spot where they would run out.

The wall was still as smooth as the black dragon's scales.

Licking my dry lips, trying to ignore my thirst, I slunk over to the other side, imitating what I'd done yesterday: watch the skies, keep to the shadows, check the other side. It was equally smooth. I gauged it a second time, despite knowing my first estimate was accurate.

I threw back my head and groaned in frustration.

A second later, I clapped my hands over my mouth.

There might've been dragons nearby who'd stayed in their caves. What if they overheard and decided to stop by for a visit in the black dragon's absence? I cursed myself and backed away from the cave mouth. I kept going until I was at the back of the cave instead. Better safe than sorry.

I faced the tunnels.

"No way out the front, but maybe the back," I muttered, feeling crazier by the second. "What do I have to lose?"

Still holding my three ropes tied together, I crept toward the back of the cave where the dark opening of the tunnel stretched tall and wide, like an open mouth ready to snap down and eat me alive.

It was large enough for the dragon to follow, if he came back.

Considering how long he'd disappeared into its depths, I could only assume it continued to be large enough within.

Swallowing, I slunk a bit farther in until it grew almost too dark to see. Though my eyes had adjusted to the dim light in the cave behind me, I had a feeling that wouldn't be the case in the tunnels. I stopped to tie the end of my rope to a big boulder on the side.

"You'll keep me grounded," I said as I tied a sturdy knot and tested it. I was talking to a rope now. Was that worse than talking to myself, or generally the same level of pitiful?

Before I took two steps, a soft thump sounded within the cave behind me.

When I glanced back, I almost choked.

I ducked behind the boulder and peered out.

A gigantic male dragon with green scales and a spiked club on the end of his tail had landed in the cave. His horns brushed the high ceiling, knocking loose rocks everywhere.

Right behind him, a gold and red dragon dropped inside, landing neatly and nuzzling him. Her smaller size and lack of horns identified her as a female. A webbed mane stretched from her forehead down her long neck and back, all the way to the tip of her tail, making her seem taller than she really was.

Their noses twitched.

They were following a scent.

My scent.

I pulled back, hoping the darkness within the tunnel would keep me hidden.

They moved fast. One moment they were at the entrance, the next they were in front of the rib cage, sniffing at the bones.

I held as still as possible, breathing shallowly.

If I got up to walk, they might see me. And then I'd be dead.

Even if they didn't notice my movement, all it would take was one misstep, to kick one little rock, and the tiniest noise would alert them to my presence immediately.

But if I *didn't* move, it was only a matter of time before their noses led them toward the back of the cave and they followed my trail here anyway.

There was no winning.

Sure enough, they were sniffing their way around the rib cage now.

Something made them lift their heads from the cave floor.

Without warning, the black dragon descended on the cave. He didn't land in the front, but flew like an arrow directly at the male and female dragons encroaching on his territory with a shriek.

The fight that broke out reminded me of a dog fight. They moved almost too fast to see, biting a tail one second, at each other's throats the next, snarling so loud that I covered my ears.

The female shrieked and dove for the black dragon's throat, while her mate attacked his wings.

Two against one.

It didn't seem fair.

But I found myself hoping the black dragon would lose—if they killed him, I could slip away down the tunnel while they tore into his body. It was a dark thought.

Better him than me.

I stepped backward, not taking my eyes off the fight, preparing to slip away.

The black dragon spun, using the momentum to knock the female into the wall with his wing before her teeth could grab hold of him, kicking out with his back feet at the same time, taking the male by surprise.

The female crashed into the cave wall, knocking huge boulders loose, which rained down on all three of them. The male ducked and escaped the brunt of the attack, but the black dragon was swift, switching to the offense in a heartbeat, forcing the green dragon to protect himself with his wings.

I jumped to the side as a rock the size of my head fell where I'd been standing.

Maybe I should run into the tunnels.

The only thing stopping me was the need to know which dragon won. That, and the fact that the pure darkness of the tunnels might slow me down, but it wouldn't bother the dragons at all.

The green dragon shrieked in pain, or maybe for his mate to get up, I couldn't tell.

The black dragon fought intelligently.

If he won, he'd know exactly where I'd gone. One look at the empty cage, and he'd be following me down the tunnel. I knew how that would end. It didn't matter how far I got. One breath of fire, and I'd be dinner.

My rib cage—and my one proven protection— was only a dozen or so paces away.

The black dragon pinned the other male against the wall.

I made my decision on instinct.

Leaving my ropes behind, I sprinted toward the bone cage.

As I ran, the female dragon came to. One cat eye blinked. In the next breath, her sharp talons arched toward me.

I swerved.

Her talon caught my bag instead.

I felt my weight shift. I was about to go down. I threw my weight forward, letting the bag fall away, leaving it behind, and kept running.

The black dragon threw himself at the female unexpectedly, slamming her into the ground. They rolled, teeth snapping.

I froze.

Between me and the rib cage stood the green dragon. He stalked toward me, smoke billowing from his nose, and his open mouth filled my vision.

I screamed and threw up my arms.

The black dragon crashed into him just before the green dragon swallowed me whole. Catching him unaware, he managed to grip the green dragon by the throat and flung him sideways, directly toward the cave opening. With a shriek of pain, the green dragon fell out the cave mouth, plummeting out of sight.

Then the black dragon was stalking the female on the other side of the cave. She hissed, arching her back.

My feet came unstuck from the cave floor and I stumbled the last few steps into the rib cage. Shoving through the bones, I tripped. The dragon-skin vest cushioned my fall.

From the ground, I stared out at them, where they circled each other.

The female retreated unexpectedly, running toward the mouth of the cave and launching off the ledge, disappearing in the same direction as her mate.

Just like that, it was over.

As the black dragon turned to face me, I forgot how to breathe.

MY BAG LAY DISCARDED on the floor just a few paces outside the cage, where the female dragon had pulled it from my back.

The black dragon folded his wings, ignoring the blood dripping from shallow scrapes, and moved toward it. He sniffed the bag, bumping it with his huge nose.

Inside was one small bit of bread and some jerky.

As the bag tipped over, the food fell out.

"Don't you dare," I cried, surprising both of us when my voice broke. "That's all I have left. You can't—" I cut off. I didn't know what the end of that sentence was. He could do what he wanted. Clenching my fists so hard that my nails broke my skin, I stepped back, chin up. "You know what? I don't care anymore."

Those cat eyes blinked at me. He raised his head slowly, still staring.

I swallowed hard. Maybe I was asking to be eaten. Maybe that's what I wanted. Starving to death was supposed to be terribly long and painful. If my father were here, he'd tell me to stop being so pessimistic. There was still hope.

I stared at the dragon, refusing to back down. Another long moment passed.

He snuffled like a horse, sounding almost as if he was speaking to me, before he swung his head around and headed into the tunnels.

Just like that, he was gone.

The beef jerky still rested where it had fallen on the ground just a few feet away.

Pursing my lips, I stared at the jerky.

"That's it."

I stepped between the bars, dashing out into the open like the little rabbit I was to him, snatched up the jerky and my bag, and scurried back inside my prison.

I ate it immediately and the bread too, along with my last gulp of water. My bag felt light as air when I strapped it back on.

In the tunnels, heavy footsteps sounded.

I looked to the back of the cave expectantly.

The dragon lumbered toward me with a small animal hanging from his mouth. All I could make out were bright pink feathers and a charred black belly. It was the size of a hen back home, but it had what looked like little horns on its head. And the feet were covered in as many feathers as the rest of the body, to the point they looked like little boots.

The dragon opened his giant maw and the bird-creature thumped lifelessly onto the cave floor. Glancing at me out of the side of his eye, he let out a great stream of fire without warning.

The bird-creature caught fire and became a ball of flames.

Another hot breath from him, this time without the inferno, and the fire vanished, leaving behind something blackened and shapeless.

Grasping it between his front teeth, the dragon tossed the cooked creature in my direction. It smacked into the bones of the rib cage before sliding down, sizzling.

With a few more growls and that infuriating pacing that put me on edge, he finished what he had to say and disappeared back into the tunnels.

The bird-creature was still smoking. I didn't dare touch it. But I stared at the offering—at least, I assumed it was an offering. The question was whether he was feeding me out of kindness or if it was a trap.

My mouth watered. As if I cared.

Once the meat no longer sizzled, I risked poking it, making sure it wouldn't burn me, before I dragged it through the bars and ripped a piece right off the bone. Taking a bite, I closed my eyes and moaned. It was delicious.

I ate every bit that I could pry off the small animal, and only as I sat licking my fingers did I start asking questions. The dragon hadn't reappeared, so if it was a trap, it must be a long-form trap. Maybe dragons liked to fatten up their prey.

Or perhaps, if they weren't terribly hungry, hunting humans became a sport. Was I only delaying the inevitable? No, I shook my head slightly at that.

I was fed and the juices had even quenched my thirst somewhat. Whatever his plan, I was in much better shape to face it now than I had been earlier.

I sighed and lay down, shivering. I pulled my legs into my body underneath the dragon skin. It helped somewhat but my arms were still bare and it would only get colder throughout the night.

When the dragon finally returned, the sun had set and the cave was nearly pitch-black, only a few stars visible in the cloudy night sky.

After he settled in with a huff, a dozen or so paces away, I stared at his dark silhouette and cleared my throat. "Thank you. For dinner."

The outline of his huge head lifted in response, but he was otherwise silent.

"You seem intelligent enough to understand, considering… everything. I suppose I could be wrong." But I didn't think I was.

A low growl emanated from his throat.

This time I was calm enough to notice that the glow of the fire in his belly didn't change. He wasn't calling up any flames. He set his head back down and I rolled onto my back, resting my hands over my full belly. "Too bad I don't speak dragon."

Another rumble, this time stretching on longer and ending with a whine.

"Sorry?" I offered.

He only snorted in response.

9

The Dragon

SHE WAS DETERMINED.

Small.

Dark hair and eyes, a fierce gaze, muscled arms and the rest of her body hidden underneath a strange coat made of green scales, muted in color, as all scales were when shed, though the musty dragon smell remained.

She shivered.

My jaws cracked open. I let my hot breath fill the cave.

Eventually her shaking stopped.

In her presence, something dormant in me began to wake. More and more, every hour I was near her.

She could save me, instinct whispered.

I huffed and swung my long neck away, curling around my body and facing away from her.

She could save me.

I scented the air. No predators lurked in the open skies. No danger besides myself.

She could save me.

Even from here, I could smell her fear mixed with boldness and a hint of something wild that I hadn't smelled in humans before.

Still, the human female hid behind fragile bone and needed to be fed like a youngling.

She could save me, the thought persisted.

It nagged at me until I couldn't ignore it.

It rang true.

I needed her for something.

The trouble was, I couldn't remember what.

1 0

Nes

WHILE THE DRAGON SLEPT, I lay on my side and stared at him in the dark. His outline made him look like a big, dark hill. His warm breath was almost soothing and my eyes grew heavy.

I woke the following morning to find him leaving once more. The ground shook slightly underfoot as he made his way to the mouth of the cave and stretched those great wings, falling out onto some unseen air current and disappearing.

I didn't waste any time. With a full belly and a good night's rest, I felt much more confident about my chances.

Ignoring the front of the cave where the slippery sides offered only a quick death, I raced toward the back, where that sweet smell lingered, and where I'd left my ropes looped over that big rock. They were still there.

I pulled the loop tight, testing it. Once confident it would hold, I ventured into the dark tunnel, using the rope as an anchor that could guide me back if I lost my way. I hesitated only once, when the tunnel curved and the last bit of light completely disappeared ahead. There was no way to know if there were other dragons hidden in the depths. I shrugged off my unease. Without flint or a candle, there was nothing I could do about that. Worrying would only slow me down.

My steps slowed anyway as the rock floor rose and dropped unexpectedly. More than once I bruised my toes or my shin on a boulder.

Another turn and the light no longer reached me at all. I slowed down even further.

That's fine, I lied to myself.

And I would keep lying to myself until I made it out alive, because the other option was curling into a heap on the rock floor and giving up.

My eyes adjusted to the deep darkness, no longer expecting to see anything, and my hearing adapted to make up for the lack.

An occasional drip sounded here and there, loud and echoing in the damp tunnels. My hand came away from the wall wet. The air was so moist that water dripped from the ceiling and formed thin, jagged spikes, both above and below.

"Ouch!" I hissed when I tripped over one of them. I moved even slower after that, sliding one foot forward, then the other, at a snail's pace. "It's fine," I repeated over and over, muttering whatever else came to mind to keep myself company.

"The ground seems to be rising," I puffed as I made my way up an incline. "Maybe I'll come out on top of a mountain. Wouldn't that be nice."

I reached the knot at the end of the first rope.

"It's fine," I whispered. It was *not* fine. How deep were these caves? "Just keep going. There are still two ropes left."

I took two more steps and the ground fell out from under me.

I screamed.

The rope burned my hands as I gripped it to stop my fall.

My shoulder banged painfully against the stone, but I stopped falling, swinging back and forth in the dark.

Everything hurt.

Panting hard, I tried to orient myself.

I couldn't see anything.

My feet weren't touching the ground. The pebbles I kicked off the wall bounced a long time before falling silent. It wasn't close.

As I scrabbled for purchase against the wall, holding on to the rope with my throbbing hands, I found a tiny ledge that let me stand.

Next, I felt above me, desperately wishing I had my harness. Instead, I looped the rope around myself as best I could, and carefully began to climb.

Climbing blind was more challenging than anything I'd ever done before.

The distance was probably only a short stone's throw, but it took ages, and by the time my fingers finally found the tunnel floor, my muscles were shaking.

When I crawled over the side and found solid ground, I lay flat on my back, taking deep breaths to calm myself.

That was unexpected.

"I made it out," I croaked. "I'm… fine." It was getting harder and harder to pretend.

Forcing myself to my knees, I crawled along the edge with extreme care, trying to find a way around the pit. It ended right beside the wall. No way to get around it on this side. Painstakingly, I felt my way along the edge of the pit in the opposite direction.

I blew out a breath of relief when it curved away and the path was clear. It didn't seem like a big hole. I began to whisper a new refrain: "I'm not dead yet…"

Once I'd safely reached the other side, I recoiled the rope around me so that I could wear them across my body.

I shivered. If I hadn't had the rope…

I'm not dead yet, I repeated once again.

Swallowing, I put my back to the hole and continued forward on hands and knees. Crawling made me even slower than before. The rocks cut into my skin and wore at my pant legs. I didn't care. It was worth it to avoid another unexpected fall.

After some time passed in the darkness, I reached the knot between the second and third rope.

I continued on.

With the way the tunnel wound this way and that, I couldn't tell if I was making progress or if I'd simply circled back in the direction I'd come.

In town, the citizens of Heechi liked to play "which is preferable" and offer a choice between two terrible options. Morbidly, I played it now. *Which would you prefer, to die under dragon fire, or to die in a dank, dark cave?* Probably the worst options anyone had ever been offered in that game. I made myself stop playing.

At the end of the third and final rope, I stopped, gripping it tightly enough that my fingers grew numb.

It was still dark.

No sign of light anywhere.

Only the sound of an occasional drip of water falling from the ceiling or my foot kicking a pebble.

I had few choices.

If I went back and tried to climb down the cliffside, I would die. If I went back to the caves with the dragon and did nothing, I would die. Or, I could let go of the rope and continue forward. And also, probably die.

But with this option, there was the smallest chance that the tunnel might lead somewhere.

That would mean setting down the rope, or tying it off somehow, and letting go.

I thought again of my game.

Dying in the front of a cave wasn't much different than dying in the back of one, except it'd be nice to have sunlight in my last days. *Not. Dead. Yet.*

I pulled out one of the two metal stakes I had left and used my small hammer to pound it into the wall.

Carefully tying the rope to the top of the stake, I made a solid knot, and then a second for good measure.

Now I had one stake and no rope.

I was angry enough with my situation that I nearly threw the useless stake away.

On my hands and knees, feeling the floor ahead of me at all times, I pressed on.

The skin on my hands and knees was beat-up and aching when the tunnel wall curved for the thousandth time and made me pause. Was it a crossroads?

I picked up a few loose rocks, throwing them in different directions, listening. If my senses could be trusted, there were at least two tunnels diverging here, maybe more.

What if they were just a big loop and I was going in circles?

I regretted coming this far.

Most of my senses were useless. Nothing to hear, nothing to see.

All I could do was keep crawling forward, in one direction or the other. I chose one at random, feeling numb.

Time passed without any way to mark it, and while it felt like hours passed, it may have been only minutes. My eyes didn't register the soft light up ahead at first.

But as I pressed forward, a light grew at the other end of the tunnel until a tiny opening appeared in the distance.

With a strangled cry of relief, I stood up and stumbled toward it. My eyes watered at the furious white light as I drew close. It shone as if it were still midday, instead of close to sunset.

That shouldn't be right.

I'd been in the caves a full day—the sun should be setting by now. I'd miscalculated time more than I'd thought.

At the tunnel entrance, my mouth fell open. My eyes must've been hungry for something other than complete darkness because the colors seemed wildly vivid. The grass sparkled a green so bright it hurt my eyes. The sky felt more familiar with the usual light blues and thin clouds, but when the sun peeked out, I could've sworn it was bigger. *How high in the cliffs am I?*

Still wearing my dragon-skin vest and my nearly empty bag, I paused just long enough to scratch a quick mark on the wall with the stake, in case I needed to find my way back, before stepping out into the clearing.

Rolling grassy hills stretched on for a short distance before a forest began and the tree line stretched ahead of me in all directions.

I pushed away the impossible questions; if I gave into them I'd lose precious time. Right now, I needed to shut down my emotions and focus on surviving.

I could figure out where I was and how to get home after I found some water.

And food.

I wasn't much of a hunter or gatherer, preferring to bring supplies with me when I ventured out on my own, but at least I had a general idea of what to do.

To find water, I needed to look for animal prints. Follow the tracks, and the beasts of the land would show you where to go. At least, that's what I'd been told.

I licked my lips and set out, trying to put all other thoughts out of my mind.

The grass appeared multicolored, as if I could pick out a dozen different shades. My eyes were confused from my time in the caves. When I reached the tree line, the same exotic range of color struck me, even in the simplest things, like the bark of trees, with deep browns all the way to soft tans. I was losing my mind.

I shook my head, blinking. I'd been alone and under pressure for far too long. It could happen to anyone trapped in a cave with a dragon for a few minutes, much less for two whole days.

Shading my eyes as I kept up a brisk walk on the mostly even ground, I followed the edge of the tree line, staying in the open, trying to judge which way was home based on the sun. I felt all turned around. Picking a general direction, I figured once the stars came out I'd know for sure, but for now I'd focus on water.

The first set of tracks I found in a patch of dirt made me pause.

What animal made these?

The pad of the foot was as large as my fist, which could be a bear. Or a mountain lion. This high up, I'd guess the latter. But instead of four claws like a lion, or five like a bear, there were six claws per foot. What kind of mutated lion was I dealing with here? Did I really want to follow a beast like that to water? It could still be there…

I gripped the stake I still held. It was sharp enough to do some damage—at close range. Swallowing the dust in my mouth, thirst won out. I stepped out in the direction of the tracks, lifting my crude weapon at the ready.

The tracks led away from the tree line over a hill into another clearing. The wide-open space was empty. I breathed a bit easier when I spied a small stream ahead. No creatures in sight.

The vivid greenish-yellow grass came up to my waist. I could hide easily enough, if need be. But so could other creatures. This thought kept me cautious. Snakes loved long grass. So did other predators.

Still, I made it to the running water without incident. The little brook was only a few paces deep and a dozen or so paces wide, with water so clear I could make out the colorful river rocks on the bottom. I wasted no time filling up my empty canteen, guzzling the entire container, and filling it again.

Refreshed, I dropped back to sit on the rocky ground beside the stream, to rest for a moment and try to form a plan. I placed the full canteen back in my bag and slung it over my shoulders and the dragon skin once more.

It was only because I was staring at my reflection, admiring the clarity of the water, that I saw the shadowy outline of a massive form rising behind me.

11

Nes

INSTINCT MADE ME LEAP to the side and roll to get as far away as possible. Just in time too. The ground shook as the attacker pounced and landed where I'd been only seconds before.

When I rolled to my hands and knees and lifted my head, I lost valuable seconds to shock.

I'd never seen anything like it. The beast's head was similar to that of an ox, with horns, a snout, and wide-set eyes as dark as onyx. The thick neck only grew wider as it met the shoulders. From there, it had a bear-like body with white fur and fierce claws as long as my fingers on each paw. It stood on two feet like a bear, but it stalked toward me with the slow grace of a lion.

I crouched too, inching backward at the same pace without taking my eyes off it.

No way I could outrun it.

My stake was useless to me, somewhere back on the ground behind the ox-beast.

Those black eyes didn't blink, didn't leave me for a second, as it closed the distance between us.

Maybe I could run toward the water—could it swim?

I remembered the hunting knife in my bag. If I could distract it long enough to pull it from my back and reach inside… A half-formed plan flashed through my mind.

Shoving forward like a sprinter at the start of a race, I hurtled toward the stream.

The beast shrieked, and the ear-splitting noise raked down my spine, lifting the hair on my arms.

I didn't look back but the ground shook as it took chase.

It reached me before I'd even hit the water.

One of those nasty claws raked down my arm, gouging deep. Only the dragon-skin vest kept those claws from ending me.

I screamed at the white-hot pain and managed to pull free, throwing my whole body to the side once more. I hoped its speed might make it less agile.

It tore past me, shrieking in fury as it missed by mere inches and plunged forward another half-dozen paces before stopping.

I yanked my bag from my back and dropped to my hands and knees, scrambling to find the hunting knife.

My hand closed around the hammer instead. Snatching it, I whirled to face the creature.

The little piece of metal looked like a toothpick when faced with the ox-beast's ferocious claws.

It stamped a foot once, twice, three times, clawing up dirt and chunks of grass, getting ready to charge.

I didn't dare take my eyes off it.

The trees were too far away. I'd never reach them in time to climb. Although I doubted that would stop this creature. And my hammer wouldn't hold up. Wouldn't even faze it.

Still, I backed up once more, holding the little hammer before me as we repeated our standoff.

The creature paused.

I took that small advantage and stepped back slowly, toward the trees, the only option I could think of.

The ox-beast crouched low.

It's stalking me.

My heart sank, but the animal didn't move forward.

If anything, it sank lower into the grass, almost as if hiding.

A whoosh overhead was my only warning.

The black dragon soared over us, so close that his tail nearly brushed my head.

A roar of fire burned the grass where the beast had been, missing it only because the animal ran toward me.

As the dragon flew around in a wide turn, the ox-beast charged.

With a squeal, I turned to run, forgetting the water behind me.

In my haste, I slipped on a wet rock and fell, smacking my head on something hard as I hit the water.

My vision turned black as the water pulled me under.

✳ ✳ ✳

A BURNING IN MY arm made me stir. I hissed as I woke, prepared to beat at the flames licking up and down my forearm, but there were none. Instead, I found dried blood in long, deep cuts from my elbow to my wrist.

The pain was unbearable.

Through my tears and the pounding in my skull from where I'd fallen, I blinked at my surroundings. I lay in the mouth of a cave, which faced the too-bright grass and too-large setting sun. On the rock wall beside me was the long scratch from my stake. The ox-beast was nowhere to be seen. I was soaking wet, but somehow I hadn't drowned.

And there was something warm behind me.

Breathing.

I tried to stay calm. Easing my head to the side, I peered over my shoulder into the shadows behind me.

Black scales.

My breath hitched and the dragon shifted in response, lifting his long neck to look at me. That yellowish eye was close enough to reach out and touch. It blinked.

I held in a squeal and shut my eyes.

How did I get here?

I lifted my lashes slightly and risked another look. Had he… rescued me? I was in the cave and safe—from the ox-beast at least. Besides the wounds along my arm and the bump on the back of my head, I didn't find any other injuries.

I didn't know what to make of it.

As harmless as the dragon seemed right now, the heat emanating from his body reminded me otherwise. Every nerve screamed to run. The terror rose inside me like ice in my veins until I was shaking.

A tear escaped and trickled down my cheek.

The dragon shifted, and I flinched.

One of his big wings opened and settled over me. It touched my side, gentle and still. The heat from being trapped between his body and the wing created a cozy cocoon and his wing felt oddly soft and warm on my skin, like a blanket.

I was more lost than ever. Should I try to run out into a strange world with creatures I'd never encountered before that might be able to kill me in a heartbeat? Or should I stay with the one creature I *knew for a fact* could.

My eyes were heavy. The pain in my arm begged me to stay still. Finally, I surrendered to the strange situation, exhausted, and closed my eyes.

When I woke, I had no idea how much time had passed. I'd nestled into the dragon in my sleep. My back was against his warm belly and his long neck stretched around and in front of me, where I had a clear view of him sleeping.

He snored lightly. I huffed at that, annoyed. Of course he didn't need to worry about predators; he was at the top of the food chain. I hadn't meant to wake him, but at my soft exhale, one of his eyes flipped open.

For a minute, we just stared at each other.

My mouth felt so dry when I opened it that I almost couldn't speak. "Why did you rescue me?"

All I got in response was a low rumble and a huff.

"Are you just waiting to eat me?" I blurted out.

He growled at that, lifting his head and giving me a distinct look of offense, eyes narrowing before he looked away as if disgusted.

"Sorry," I mumbled. "I just don't get it. You know you're not really following dragon etiquette, right?"

A bit of tooth showed at that.

"Is that… a smile?" I asked, incredulous.

His tail swished and he ignored me.

"I'm going to take that as a yes." For some reason, the one-sided conversation was making me feel better. I was truly losing my mind if I was taking comfort in a dragon.

Still, the side of me that my mother always disapproved of pushed me onward. I moved to sit, carefully cradling my injured arm and wincing.

He pulled his wing back, retracting it against his side and out of my way.

I held my non-injured arm out for balance as I tried to stand, but I swayed and fell against him. Instinct made me tense.

He didn't attack. Only blinked at me.

"Sorry," I managed to say. My body was weak; I didn't know if I could stand on my own. "Hope you don't mind."

He didn't move for a long moment. Then he shook his head.

"I knew you could understand me," I muttered, more to myself than anything. My fingertips brushed against those black scales. He twitched slightly where I touched him. "You can feel that?" I glanced at him.

Another slow nod.

I pressed my whole palm against him, petting almost like I would a horse. The scales were deceptively soft and warm. I shouldn't have been surprised, considering I wore the skin a dragon had shed and had experienced firsthand the flexibility. Yet it was so different on a living, breathing dragon. Especially when I only needed to reach a bit farther to place my hand over the glowing warmth of his chest where fires flared and died down at any given moment.

I shifted away from him slightly, but the extra foot of space made me shiver. I'd always been near sweating in his presence before, so that alone caught my attention and worried me. Twisting my arm to get a better look at the damage, I bit my lip at the pain. Another shiver reinforced my fear. The wound was causing a growing fever. I felt dizzy.

Without letting myself think about it too hard, I scooted back toward the dragon until I could lean against him. I sighed in relief at the warmth.

His eyes were still on me. It was unnerving.

"Don't stare."

He only blinked.

"It's rude." I moved to cross my arms, but quickly halted at the sharp sting. I clutched the wounded arm to my chest and endured the throbbing, trying to distract myself. "My name is Nesrin, by the way. My family calls me Nes. I need a name to call you by."

He growled a nonsensical response.

"Sure," I nodded sagely. "We could go with that, or, since I might have trouble saying it, we could try something else. What about Firebreather?"

He snarled.

"Okay, okay, you don't love it." I held up my uninjured hand in understanding. "What about Doost?" I asked after a second, adding, "It means friend…"

Our eyes met. I struggled to hold his gaze, swallowing hard.

He gave me one of his slow nods.

My mouth slowly stretched into a grin. Too bad I couldn't sell a dragon to pay our debt instead of an egg, because this show would be a huge hit.

1 2

The Dragon

FRIEND.

Something told me I'd had friends once.

The word meant something.

* * *

IT CAME BACK TO me in pieces.

A memory of tower walls, jarring white.

A woman with deep ebony hair, pale skin, and eyes equally pale, like the sky on a cloudless day.

Pain.

Not physical hurt, but emotion. Strange and unfamiliar, I didn't immediately recognize it.

An old friend, tugging on his vest to straighten it, long black hair swept back. A small smile and nod, before he trailed me down a long corridor, guarding me.

We'd been close. His name escaped me.

My own name escaped me.

* * *

THE GIRL SHIFTED IN her sleep.

Nesrin.

It was the only name I knew.

That dormant part of me whispered it over and over, reminding me. No longer sleeping, it demanded to be heard.

Remember.

A soft moan drew my attention. Her face scrunched in pain.

I lurched to my feet, padding to the front of the cave, driven by instinct. Food. I would bring food.

* * *

AWAY FROM HER, I remembered little.

But by her side, the trickle of memories became a flood. Disjointed, but growing clearer.

The beast in me withdrew, just a bit.

With so much still shrouded in mystery, one focus took over, as much by impulse as choice: *keep her alive.*

13

Nes

MY ARM GREW WORSE.

Doost brought me another animal to eat, but I couldn't manage more than a few bites.

I woke to find a mammoth moon overhead; when I blinked, it was light out.

I'm losing time.

My body shook with cold even when I pressed into his side.

The fever was getting worse.

It was odd for a wound to get infected so quickly. Almost otherworldly.

"I'm so thirsty," I managed to tell him when I felt more lucid.

His long nose dipped down toward me and I could've sworn he looked concerned.

"Back at the stream, my bag is still there somewhere…" I trailed off. Maybe it wasn't.

Did I fill my canteen?

I couldn't remember.

My wound needed cleaning. And a bandage. Maybe after a short nap…

I drifted to sleep and woke feeling like a block of ice.

Doost was returning with something in his mouth. My bag.

"Thank you," I whispered, pulling out the canteen from inside, which was blessedly full.

I drank deeply.

Sleep claimed me again.

I didn't know how much time had passed when Doost nudged me gently with his nose. The sun shone in and should've warmed me, but nothing could pierce the cold in my bones, except where my arm burned fiercely, as if it lay directly in a fire.

With one long talon, Doost scratched a line in the cave wall, curving it into what looked oddly enough like a letter. Then again, and again, and again. *STAY.*

I wanted to laugh at that. "Do I look up to going anywhere?" I mumbled, closing my eyes.

"How do you know how to write?" I asked a few minutes later, but when I peered out from under my lashes, he was gone.

A dragon who knew how to write a human language. Interesting.

Between shivering and dreams, I imagined an entire conversation with the dragon.

"Doost, you're a strange one, you know that right?"

"How rude." He lifted his chin in offense.

"I'm just stating the obvious."

In my dream state, we both chuckled.

"Do all dragons know how to spell? Is there some sort of dragon school?" I asked.

His yellow eyes were turning brown. They seemed so human and warm and reminded me of my father's eyes.

"Don't be ridiculous," he snorted. That's exactly what my father would say. And I knew he was right. Dragons couldn't read and write.

"You're not a normal dragon, are you?" I mumbled to Doost.

When I looked over, he'd morphed into my brother. "What kind of question is that, Nes?" Roohstam rolled his eyes. "I thought you were smart, little sister."

"Shut up, Roohstam," I threw my pillow at him. "I'm smarter than you." When he didn't answer, I rolled back over to see where he went and was met with an empty pile of rocks instead. *Where did Roohstam go?*

I shifted to look and rolled onto my arm. With a hiss of pain, my memories came back.

Groaning, I cradled my arm, trying not to touch the angry red wounds crusted with greenish-yellow scabs.

I couldn't stay in this cave; I needed a healer.

My eyes were drawn against my will to the jagged scratches on the wall: *STAY.* I shook my head. So it *had* been real.

I felt lucid now, but I wasn't sure how long that would last.

If I stayed here, I didn't know if I'd ever leave.

Against his orders, I decided to go.

I pulled myself onto my knees, leaning on my good arm. Staggering to my feet, I tried to walk but the room spun and I dropped back to the cave floor.

I tried to crawl on my knees and good arm instead, letting the bad one dangle.

The jolting movement set a new fire ablaze, opening my scabs for fresh blood to leak out.

I sank to the ground only a few feet from where I'd begun, exhausted.

I supposed I'd stay here after all. And without food, water, or a way to deal with my infection, probably die here. The thought should've bothered me more than it did. But all I could think about was how tired I was. So tired…

* * *

I DIDN'T HEAR DOOST return. It was only when he dropped something wet and warm on my injured arm that I roused from sleep with a scream of agony.

"No, no!" I yelled at him, throwing off the sticky green mass. The fire licked down my arm and renewed throbbing filled my senses. Tears of pain streamed from my eyes despite my best efforts to hold them in. When I blinked them away, the cave was dark now that the sun had set.

Besides the glow of fire in Doost's belly, everything else was dim.

"Don't touch, please!" My voice was hoarse from pain.

He moved to scoop up the green stuff again. It looked like some kind of plant, chewed up to the point that I didn't recognize it.

"Don't touch," I repeated.

His huge form rose over me.

"No. No. No!" I screamed, and he roared in response. "I don't want it!" I yelled as he dropped the thick strands of green onto my wounds once more and stepped on my arm with his huge foot, holding whatever it was in place.

He wasn't setting his full weight on me or my arm would've snapped like a twig, but it still felt as if a mountain had crashed down on my limb.

I sobbed in pain.

"Why are you doing this?" I cried between heaving breaths. "I thought you liked me. Why are you trying to kill me? What kind of torture is this?" I moaned and thrashed under his weight but to no avail.

His roars pierced my ears, and I fought on, refusing to give up, wrenching my shoulder painfully.

It burned.

Gasping, I gave up.

It took a few more panted breaths before it occurred to me that my arm felt numb more than anything else.

Did he cut off circulation? I tried to pull away weakly once more, which sent shooting fire down my shoulder, and gave up.

"I think you've crushed it."

He growled something, and didn't move for another full minute while I lay there gasping for breath, trying to recover.

A cooling sensation spread from the soft, wet stuff on my arm. The pain faded, replaced by relief. It reminded me of a human remedy we used in the village for burns and cuts that fought infection.

I vaguely felt him remove his weight from my arm as I drifted off to sleep once more, sinking into the respite from the pain.

✳ ✳ ✳

"DOOST, YOU BIG BULLY," I groaned as I lay there the next morning. My arm was better. Much better. "Why didn't you tell me this was the *kushta* herb? I wouldn't have fought so hard."

His tail swished in annoyance and his eyes turned to slits as he glared at me.

My body still ached, but I could already feel it improving as it fought the infection. I'd never experienced such an accelerated sickness before. The thought nagged at me. Something about it hadn't seemed normal.

I stayed on the ground, arm stretched out where it'd been since the night before, letting chewed-up greens and dragon spit do its work. "Okay, yes. You tried to tell me," I acknowledged. "To be fair, your accent is a little hard to understand."

He huffed and stood to pace toward the entrance. I thought for a moment I'd offended him, but he paced back, walking a track that seemed familiar, as if he'd walked it many times before. *Had he been up all night?*

"I'll be fine," I reassured him. Part of me wanted to shake my head at the idea of reassuring a dragon. "I just need a little time, that's all." And some food and water. And maybe some fresh herbs and something to wrap my arm so I could be up and about while it worked.

"How do you know a human medicinal herb anyway?" I asked as I tugged at my bag, pulling it closer until I could reach inside and take out my canteen. Unscrewing it with one hand was difficult. When I glanced over at him, he stopped pacing to growl, but of course, I didn't understand a word.

"Okay, okay, let me guess." I waved my good hand to pacify him, "I can figure this out…"

He left his track to come settle in front of me like a cat, curling up and waiting, those watchful eyes unblinking.

I drank the rest of my water and set down the canteen, staring up at the ceiling of the cave where long stalactites had formed. "Were you hatched and raised by humans?" I guessed. That would explain why he hadn't killed me yet.

But Doost only shook his big head, not bothering to lift it from the floor.

"Okay…" I mulled over what other options there might be. "I bet you fly over human villages and study them."

Again, he shook his head and turned away with a grumble of frustration.

I frowned. *What else could it be?* "Do dragons use the herb too?" I asked after a few minutes of silence.

Doost growled at that, not looking at me as he got up to return to his track, pacing toward the front of the cave and back, to the front and back.

My stomach growled in response. "Fine, I'll stop guessing," I bargained in a syrupy tone, "if you'll bring me some dinner?"

In a huff, he spread his wings to their full length, filling the cave opening and blocking out light completely for a split second before they beat the air in silent, deadly strokes and carried him away.

"Thanks. I'll see you later," I mumbled at his receding shape in the sky. "No, no, you don't need to say a long goodbye, or tell me when you'll be back. I'll be fine."

With a sigh, I rolled onto my back once more to stare at the roof of the cave, careful not to jostle my arm. What an odd situation this was. I'd be willing to bet no one else in history had ever experienced a dragon for a nurse.

* * *

WHEN HE RETURNED WITH another large bird and cooked it for me, I didn't have time to tease him. I was too busy blowing on the steaming leg so it would be cool enough to eat.

I held my injured arm as still as possible. The herbs had dried at this point and flaked off when I moved, revealing the damaged skin underneath.

Doost was pacing yet again, but at the sight of it, he took off into the depths of the tunnel.

"I'm in awe of your communication skills," I told the black hole behind me. "Thanks for telling me where you're going."

An echo of a growl reached me and I laughed a little to myself as I finished the rest of my meal and, when it was all gone, licked my fingers clean. I'd eaten every bite of the strange bird. My belly was bursting. *Who knows when my next meal might be?*

Peeling back the rest of the dried herbs, I surveyed the damage to my arm. The deep cuts were a much healthier color today than they'd been the day before. They'd scabbed over easily. But some of the herbs had gotten embedded in it, and as the crust fell away, the wound reopened. I sucked in a breath as the last bit came away, gritting my teeth against the pain. It throbbed a little, but was nothing compared to before.

Still, I wasn't out of the woods yet. I needed to clean it. The closest pool of water was the stream I'd come from the day before.

That thought brought back everything that had happened the day before—no... I counted again... two days before—when the strange animal had attacked me. *What kind of creature was that?*

Part of me was convinced I'd imagined it. If not for the claw marks on my arm, I wouldn't have believed it. I'd never seen an animal quite like it, which meant we must've been quite a bit farther from home than I'd originally thought.

The more important question, though, was did the creature live by the stream? Or was it safe to go there and wash my arm?

I walked to the mouth of the cave without any difficulty and stared out at the strange clearing. The colors were still more vivid than back home. Just a few steps away, my eyes caught on some pink flowers I hadn't noticed before. They were shaped like an open mouth. A fly landed on one, and it snapped shut, effectively trapping it inside. I shivered. *Even the flowers are aggressive.* I definitely wasn't in Heechi anymore.

I bit my lip, staring aimlessly at the strange trees and fields before me. *How long have I been gone?* I tried to count the days, first the ones climbing, then in the cave, then here... My family had to be worried sick.

Thinking of them made my eyes burn.

I shook my head. Worrying over my father and whether or not his trip had succeeded was useless. It would only distract me here. And distractions could be fatal. I stared harder at the landscape, silently daring any creatures to try attacking me now.

The burning in my arm came back with a vengeance as I waited for Doost. The sun reached the highest point in the sky and began to make its descent and still he didn't appear.

Finally, I shook my head in frustration and stepped out of the cave, heading toward the water. I needed to wash my wounds or the infection would return.

Grabbing my bag, I followed yesterday's path to the water. It wasn't as far as I'd thought. No creatures appeared, no unexpected surprises. After satisfying my thirst and filling my canteen, I eyed the surrounding area carefully before I bent down by the edge. Cupping water in my hand, I trickled a tiny amount over my arm. "Ow! Ah! That burns!" I threw my head back and blew out a breath. Better to just get it over with.

Wading into the water up to my knees, I bent down and submerged my entire arm. I nearly screamed at the pain, holding it in with clenched teeth and a moan. I felt lightheaded. I didn't move, didn't scrub the wound or try to rinse it, just let the moving water run past me where I knelt and focused on staying upright.

The initial pain faded and the icy water cooled off the burning sensation. It was such a relief that I didn't move for a long time, until my entire body felt frozen.

Splashing out of the water, I dropped to the ground and lay flat on my back in the warm sun, drying off. The sun was beginning to set. *I should head back.*

I wasn't even halfway to the cave when Doost dropped from the sky, hurtling down as if he'd been shot. The impact on the ground made it vibrate under my feet. He ran up to me and spat green strands of *kushta* at my feet before roaring directly in my face. His hot breath was moist and smelled like raw meat.

I coughed and spun away. "What in the name of Jinn are you doing?" I yelled, which earned me another fierce roar.

He stalked around me in a circle, pacing to show his frustration.

"You were gone!" I snapped, waving my good hand in the air. "What was I supposed to do?" I swallowed, lifting my chin. "I needed a drink."

He growled and stalked away to the stream behind me. While he drank, I knelt to scoop up the *kushta* a little bit at a time. He'd chewed it into almost a paste. I wrinkled my nose as I slathered it across my arm until it was just one big mass of green goo. As disgusting as it was, it felt so good that I didn't stop until I had a thick layer. The relief came quickly.

As the pain receded, my mind grew clearer. I wanted to wrap the arm so the paste wouldn't fall off. The prairie grass surrounding me was tall and thick. I snapped off one stalk at a time, painstakingly wrapping it around and around, covering the end with a new stalk each time it ran out, until it spanned from my elbow to my wrist. I tucked the tail end of the grass underneath to hold it in place.

Doost had returned, watching the process with a disapproving eye, though he didn't protest.

"Thank you for the herbs."

He huffed again, but his head lifted to a more relaxed state. When he tilted it toward the caves, I knew exactly what he meant, but I argued anyway. "What if we didn't sleep in the caves tonight?" I begged. After so many nights within their depths, I was beginning to feel suffocated. "I want to see the stars."

He'd already begun shaking his big head, but at the mention of the stars, he paused. Then, a slow nod.

"Okay, it's a deal." I was immediately more cheerful. The only thing missing from my plan was dinner. Maybe I could dig up some edible roots by the stream. Since we were still close, I stood to scrounge around.

Doost followed me like a puppy.

"What do you normally do when you come here?" I said aloud, though he couldn't answer. As I walked I studied the ground and added, "I mean, you've come here the last few nights, right? Is this where you're from?"

He nodded.

"Do all the caves lead here?"

I thought I was onto something, but he shook his head.

"Huh… just yours?" I frowned, digging up a root I didn't recognize. I tossed it over my shoulder. Better to go hungry than accidentally eat something harmful. "That's odd. So, you're from here, but none of the other dragons are."

He only huffed a sigh.

I dug up another plant I didn't recognize, with a strange red bulb on the bottom and long, feather-like leaves above the surface. I held it out in frustration. "Why is everything different here? How am I supposed to know what to eat?"

It was a rhetorical question. I threw the strange root away like the previous. Doost stepped up to look at it, snuffling, before he took a bite and swallowed it whole. He turned to look at me, as if to say, "See? It's fine."

"Thanks, I appreciate the effort," I said, moving on as I rolled my eyes. "But human digestion and dragon digestion are two very different things. I'd rather not risk it."

He snarled at me, ears flat against his head. Digging up another feather-leafed plant with his teeth, he tossed it in my direction, bulb first. It nearly hit me in the face.

I held up my hands to pacify him. "Okay, I see your point. You did know about the herbs for my arm."

I followed the plant to where it had landed on the ground, a bit smushed now, and held it up to show him. "I'll give it a shot, but this is on you if I keel over and die."

He only snorted at my dramatics.

The outside of the bulb was crunchy but the inside was white and surprisingly juicy.

"Mmm," I said in approval. "Good choice. At least if I die, I'll die happy."

His lip curved on one side and a tooth showed.

I giggled at that strange smile. "I'm just happy to be out of that cave. Good riddance."

That earned me a flick of his ear. He dug out more and more of the strange plants for me to eat. "Enough, enough," I said after a dozen. "There's no way I'll eat that many."

Another flick of the ear. He scooped up a mouthful of the ones he'd just uprooted, crunching them in a few bites before swallowing.

"Ah, of course, my misunderstanding." I gathered up a few more for myself, and he ate the rest. "I didn't know dragons ate vegetables," I spoke with my mouth full. "Or is that only you as well?"

He confirmed his uniqueness with yet another slow nod. He crept closer, eyes on mine, intent.

"I feel like you're trying to tell me something," I said as I pulled off my bag to place the remaining root vegetables inside. "I just don't know what."

A rumbling sounded in his chest and he continued to stare, but it gave me no clue.

"Maybe I should learn to speak dragon." I lifted a hand to shade my eyes from the setting sun. "Is there a good place to watch the sunset around here?"

I didn't really expect a dragon to have formed an opinion on something like that and took off in the direction of a tall hill without waiting for a responding growl.

At the top of the ridge, my jaw dropped. There was a shimmer on the horizon, like a mirage or a ghostly fog. As the sun slipped into it, it glistened and sparkled like gold dust in the air.

"Where *are* we?" I asked, more to myself than him.

He perked up at the question, ears flicking forward in anticipation. "This isn't anywhere near Heechi at all, is it?"

He swung his head from side to side and a growl came out as if he couldn't help it.

An odd thought struck me. The too-bright colors, the strange creatures, the way the sun and moon were too large, as if they were closer than they'd been before. "Is this... Are we even in human lands?"

As soon as I asked it, I wished I could take it back.

Even more so when he shook his head again, slower this time.

The blood drained from my face as my eyes grew wide. I knew the answer, but I still had to ask.

"Are you telling me... are we in *Jinn*?"

14

The Dragon

EACH QUESTION BROUGHT ANSWERS, not just for the girl, but for me.

Memories triggered.

"I'm sorry," a woman's voice had whispered in my dreams. Or had it been in my ear? Her voice trembled but didn't break. "It has to be done."

A stretching then, of limbs, muscle, bone. Joints snapping painfully. Changing. Screams turning to roars. Roars becoming fire.

Once the pieces of memory surfaced, they were mine. But the depths held so much more. I sensed it.

A crown.

It was a curling white gold, simple. Lighter than a hunk of metal should be, thanks to Jinni magic flowing through it. Stronger too. Even when I was young, I'd felt its energy.

The more Nesrin's questions brought answers, the more a direction began to call to me.

I knew, somehow, what I would find if I flew that direction. A full explanation of what had happened to me—no, that wasn't quite it.

The *source*.

For the first time I could remember, I felt fear.

1 5

Nes

I SHOOK MY HEAD in denial even as he nodded, deep and unmistakable. "No, it can't be. That doesn't make any sense. Humans can't get into Jinn. The entrance is secret and forbidden. How did you—? How did I—? This doesn't make sense," I repeated, knowing I sounded like an idiot. "Why would you bring me to Jinn?"

When I swiveled my head to glance at him, he ignored me, not deigning to answer.

"Right, you didn't."

I faced the sunset again. Its warmth touched my face until it slipped out of sight, leaving a fading orange glow behind.

When Doost lay down, I sat beside him. It was strange to be so close to a lifelong enemy. I didn't know why I trusted him. Sometimes when he shifted in the corner of my eye, I'd flinch. But while I avoided touching him, I always stayed close. There were predators here in Jinn that I'd never faced, while the predator by my side no longer alarmed me. I frowned, unsure if that was a good thing or not. Resting my arms on my knees, we watched the sky grow gray until the first star twinkled through, followed by another and another.

"Wow." I breathed a sigh of appreciation and stretched out on the hill to lie with my hands behind my head, staring up at the thousands of stars above, more brilliant than I'd ever seen. "They seem so much bigger here," I told Doost.

He curled up beside me, reminding me again of a cat—aloof, but secretly paying attention.

"It makes sense. I should've known this was Jinn the moment I stepped out of the cave."

His growl sounded sleepy. Minutes later, he was snoring loud enough that I couldn't sleep. I lay there trying to find well-known constellations, too awestruck to sleep anyway. Nothing was familiar.

The only Jinni I'd ever met was Joram, the Jinni my father had hired right before he left town.

They didn't come to Heechi.

I knew the rumors—our people didn't like them, and they didn't like us. I'd never thought to ask why.

But like most citizens in Heechi, I'd assumed the stories of a race whose home was in the heavens was a myth. The Jinn were just Gifted men taking advantage of superstitious folk. Or at least, that's what I'd thought.

Now, of course, that theory was shattered by the knowledge that Jinn wasn't a make-believe place at all.

It was extremely real.

As I lay there letting that sink in, the night air grew cold enough to make me shiver. When a breeze

BETHANY ATAZADEH

made the hair on my arms lift and my teeth chatter, I glanced over at the giant furnace in dragon form just a half dozen paces away.

I hesitated.

His body was as big as two huge draft horses put together, his long neck and tail the size of tree trunks, and between his body and his tail was a space just large enough to curl up in. Scooting closer to Doost's side, I eased myself over his tail, into the space between it and his belly. I held my breath.

He didn't react. His smoky breath remained even. And warm.

Lying back down, I shifted slowly in the small space, trying not to touch him. In his sleep, Doost shifted, tucking his tail closer until it pressed against me, nudging me into his side.

I peeked at him from under my eyelashes.

He seemed to be unconscious.

I couldn't bring myself to get up. He was so warm. I shook my head slightly and closed my eyes. *I still can't believe I'm trusting a dragon. If my family could only see me now.*

* * *

"THERE'S SOMETHING I NEED to ask," I said after we'd gone through our routine of Doost bringing breakfast and watching me burn my fingers as I tried to eat too fast.

When he'd moved unexpectedly to meet my gaze, I didn't flinch. I even found myself standing closer to him than I used to. I pursed my lips and shook my head at that. Taking another long drink of water, I refilled my canteen in the stream, stalling.

He waited. Resting on the top of the ridge with his wings spread out to soak up the sun, head up and neck arched to stare down at me. He was truly majestic.

I cleared my throat. "Why did you take me that day?" I knew he couldn't answer, and tried to find better words as I fiddled with the wrap on my arm, which felt remarkably improved. In fact, the cut itself was only superficial. It wouldn't have caused more than a slight irritation back home; yet it had almost killed me here. More evidence that Jinn was a dangerous place.

His growl sounded like he was truly trying to speak, but of course, I understood none of it. I needed to ask a yes or no question.

My words came out stilted. "You're not like other dragons, are you?"

When he shook his head, I released a breath I didn't know I'd been holding. "I was never supposed to be dinner."

It wasn't a question, but he shook his head again anyway.

"I don't understand." I threw my hands in the air. "What kind of dragon doesn't kill people? It's unnatural. It's like you're not a real dragon at all—"

Doost lunged to his feet, circling me. His growls made the hair on my arms lift instinctually, despite the way I'd begun to trust him.

"I didn't mean to offend. Of course, you're a real dragon, I know that—"

Again he cut me off, thumping his heavy tail on the ground and shaking his head so violently, I had to jump back or risk being knocked over.

"You're… not a real dragon?" I said slowly.

Doost met my eyes and dipped his head in a careful, exaggerated nod, so I couldn't miss it.

"What are you then?" I whispered, more to myself than anything, as I stared at his black scales, wings, and tail for some clue. "Is that why you dragged me up to your lair?" I mumbled, frowning. "Were you trying to show me something?"

He stood, wings folding in and extending again in his excitement.

I perked up. "You were?"

He lowered his head to my level until he was less than an arm's length away. His eyes met mine—unblinking, hopeful.

"I'm onto something," I said for his benefit, and didn't need his huge nod to know it was true. "Have you already showed me and I missed it?"

This time it was no.

"Well…" I shrugged, waving a hand for him to lead on. "Whenever you're ready then."

I wasn't sure what I expected. Maybe a short walk down a trail. Or for him to take his true form right there, perhaps as an ox-beast in disguise.

He crouched down, lowering his entire body to the ground, including his neck, and waited.

"You want me to—? No, I'm sorry, that first flight was my limit." I shook my head and would've crossed my arms but the makeshift bandages got in the way. "I'll walk."

His eyes narrowed, and he didn't move.

"It can't be that far," I argued.

I loved the heights when I was in control, but he was suggesting an entirely different experience.

A low growl rumbled in his belly.

His wing stretched out and scooped me toward him until my hands touched the side of his neck.

Pressed against his warm scales, my heart thudded.

Am I really doing this?

I swallowed. I'd faced death so many times in the last few days. *What's one more time?*

I opened my mouth to agree, but it was too dry for words.

Instead, I put my foot into the cleft where his wing met his body, using it like a stepping stool to climb onto his back, swinging a leg over his neck.

He stood before I was ready and I slipped.

"Wait, stop, ah!" I slid toward his right wing.

He stilled, holding himself carefully level as I wedged my foot in the curve between his wing and his body.

Pushing off the wing, I scrambled back up his side to my original seat and straddled his neck once more.

"What am I supposed to hold on to?" I tried to wrap my hands around his thick neck but the moment he shifted I lost my grip. "I can't do this. I can't even ride bareback on our family horse, so there's no way I'm risking this."

He swung his head around to glare at that.

"I'm not comparing you to a horse, stop getting so worked up." I rolled my eyes, but paused, biting my lip in thought. "Actually, that's not a bad idea."

I shrugged out of the dragon-skin vest that I still wore, replacing my bag. The scales were flexible and strong—if I could loop them around his neck, they could almost function as makeshift reins to keep me stable. It was worth a try.

Swinging the vest around his neck, I tried to grab the other side, but failed.

Doost bent to take it and bring it up to me.

His lip curled back for me to grab it. I'd never seen his fangs so close before.

The point glistened razor sharp in the sunlight.

I gulped.

Carefully, I stretched my fingers to grasp the skin and he let go.

I gripped the tether tighter. My arm twinged at the extra effort, but I ignored it; my life depended on not letting go.

Scooting forward, I leaned against his neck and stretched the length of my body down his back.

My knuckles turned white where I clutched the dragon skin. "Okay," I whispered. "I'm ready."

He launched from the ground without warning.

I screamed.

Eyes squeezed shut, I held on until my fingers screamed in pain as his great wings flapped soundlessly.

I took a shuddering breath, waiting to fall off, but we leveled out within a few beats.

After a bit longer, I began to adjust to the movement, swaying with the ups and downs.

Opening my eyes, I gasped.

The ground stretched so far away that the scenery looked like a map from my father's office; the trees were a mass of green, and the rivers mere squiggly lines.

We flew through clouds and mist soaked my skin as everything became white and hazy.

When we broke through the veil, my lips parted.

A castle rose before us like nothing I'd ever seen. Every angle was sharp as a blade. Its spires rose in pointed white peaks with light blue turrets.

Surrounding the enormous castle were fields of soft lavender flowers interspersed with pure white trees that looked like puffy dandelions from this distance.

A deep pool of water curved around the castle aimlessly, like a strange path with multiple trails.

As we flew over it, our reflection rippled along the surface. Doost's massive wingspan, with his outstretched neck and long tail flowing behind him, appeared on the water like an oddly shaped bird, while I was too small to be visible.

The wind in my ears was loud. I didn't try to speak.

Doost circled the castle with a beautiful courtyard that stretched as far as I could see.

A tall fountain stood in the center of the gardens, with tiny walking paths around it and all kinds of plants too small to make out.

As Doost flew, he swung his head around to stare at me, then the fountain, then at me again.

I would've pointed in question, but was too terrified to let go of the reins.

He made yet another pass, still too high to make out if there were people in the gardens, before aiming for the outer edges right near the castle wall.

We set down near the outer wall and I nearly fell in my haste to dismount.

My legs wouldn't hold me up. I knelt until I could regain my balance and catch my breath.

"Let's not do that again," I said between gasps, pulling the dragon skin back on. "If I have one more heart-stopping experience, I think my body will give out."

He didn't even growl in response, only stared in the direction of the fountain, like a statue.

I took a few more deep breaths, admiring the gardens. The landscaping was impeccable. Everything was so neatly groomed that not a single stray blade of grass grew too long. Wherever the shrubbery grew tall and thick, it was clearly trained into form, twisting here and there, creating unique designs.

The perfectly sculpted gray-and-white brick wall stretched ahead of us, curving out of sight. I knew from my aerial view that it surrounded the castle, the gardens, and then some. From this vantage point, it stretched taller than Doost and made me feel small, like a little kitten in the stables back home that could get trampled by a single misplaced hoof.

This was Jinn, after all. Rumor said the Jinn would grant your every wish. Others said they stole your wishes and made them their own, leaving you an empty shell. I didn't know what to believe, but I'd meant it when I told Doost I'd reached my limits. I didn't want to be here.

"What do you need me to see?" I asked, dusting off my hands as I stood. "Let's get it over with. This place is unnerving."

He blinked for the first time since we'd arrived. Almost as if he'd forgotten I was there. *Is he nervous too?* That didn't make me feel better.

He set a slow pace through the gardens, eyes watchful, head low. The path curved, but was always wide enough for Doost. The soft wood chips crunched under his claws and my boots. Some of the plants and trees were familiar, but others caught my attention.

I admired the strange albino trees sprinkled throughout the gardens. Their elegant branches swept straight up to the sky and looked almost like a candelabra with a million different candlesticks.

Pink flowers covered every open space, like an ocean of cherry blossoms. The huge fountain rose above the trees, taller than a two-story building, visible long before we reached it.

I didn't see any animals, which struck me as odd once I noticed the silence they left behind.

Even so, I wasn't too worried until Doost paused at the curve in the road before we reached the fountain.

He pushed away the pretty wood shavings that lined the path, to get to the dirt underneath. He scratched painstakingly careful letters into the dark soil. It took two tries to make it legible.

HIDE.

"What? Where?" I protested. "What's going to happen that you can't take care of me?" I crossed my arms, laughing a little.

Doost clawed through the word, making it unreadable before he raked the mulch back over top of it and stared at me.

I stopped laughing. "You're serious."

He bared his teeth at me, fangs glistening. The growl was soft and deep in his throat, but menacing, and those expressive ears were flat against his head.

"Okay, yes, I'm going to… hide somewhere. Jinni's honor."

He stopped snarling, but didn't move.

"Oh. Right now? Okay, right." I shook my head at him, muttering to myself as I stepped off the path into the undergrowth, weaving my way between the trees, admiring the beautiful white ones that popped up now and then. "He wants to show me something, but wants me to just figure it out on my own. Very helpful. Not at all confusing." I knew he could hear me, even when I spoke under my breath, but there was no answering growl.

I cut off, starting to worry in earnest. *What in all the lands could scare a dragon?*

I headed through the underbrush in the same general direction as we had been before, toward the fountain. The tip of it was visible from within the trees. Doost's heavy footsteps sounded along the path nearby, drowning out any crunch of leaves under my feet.

When I neared the edge and glimpsed the path ahead, I slowed. I found a place where the trees and underbrush were thick, affording me a hiding place with a good view of the fountain. It was even more beautiful up close.

Five tiers of pools caught water as it cascaded down, from the tiniest birdbath at the top, to a pool that would take a full minute to swim across at the base.

I wasn't much of a swimmer, but the soothing trickle seemed so refreshing I was tempted to climb in. The only thing stopping me was Doost as he rounded the path. Having taken the long way, he lumbered up to the fountain with his head lowered and ears back, almost submissive, except for the way his tail whipped back and forth with a held back fury.

What's he waiting for? He stood by the fountain for so long I was getting ready to step out of hiding when out of nowhere another human flashed into existence right in front of him.

No, not a human. A Jinni.

16

Nesrin

WITH HER BACK TO me, at first all I could make
out was her long black hair that flowed freely with a
touch of gray streaking through it. As she turned to
face the fountain, a ray of sunlight caught the top of
her head and something sparkled. A crown.

Her dress shimmered with Jinni magic that made
my skin tingle. It changed colors as the light touched
it, glittering gold and tight-fitting on top, but cut open
along her legs for movement. Those pale legs were
brazenly bare beneath the fabric, besides the
strappings of gold sandals that wove around her
calves. When she spoke, her voice carried. "Hello,
darling. I've missed you."

Doost didn't fight her when she reached out to
touch his nose. Her hand rested there and then caressed
his cheek. So familiar.

Is it commonplace to pet a dragon in Jinn? I
blinked at that, doubtful. Even a Jinni should be far
more concerned about proximity to a beast his size—
the fact that she wasn't spoke volumes. I remembered
his revelation earlier, that he wasn't really a dragon at

all. Did this Jinni know that? Another thought hit me. Was she the *reason* he was a dragon? I shrank back into the foliage, understanding Doost's demand for secrecy more by the second.

His ears pressed back even farther until barely discernable against his scales, but he didn't bare his teeth at her. The fire in his chest remained subdued.

Jewels on her fingers, wrists, and neck caught the sunlight as she gestured to someone behind her. *Is this… Could she be the queen of Jinn?* It would explain the crown, but not what she was doing here or why she was talking to a dragon.

A large wolf strode from the forest at her beckoning.

Doost and the likely-queen only stood waiting.

The wolf padded up beside the woman and she rested a possessive hand on his head.

"My spies informed me you've found a portal to the human world," she said, standing between the two beasts as if in an everyday conversation. She sighed. Moving away from them, she strode to the lip of the marble fountain, her back to me. "Each time I think we've found the last *Daleth,* another appears."

Doost lowered his head toward the wolf, angling in an unspoken question.

The wolf wouldn't meet his eye; instead it moved to a spot near the woman and curled up on the grass, ignoring them.

She turned then, finally giving me a good view of her regal face with perfectly arched brows and dark, kohl-lined eyes. When she smiled, she was

BETHANY ATAZADEH

breathtaking. "Don't worry, darling. I've already forgiven you for leaving, even temporarily."

Doost huffed.

"I know, I know. You had to try," the woman said, closing the space between them, taking his head in her hands once more. "I'd assumed your animal nature would distract you. You're stronger than I thought."

Doost let her draw him down to her eye level. His ears flicked wildly with some emotion I couldn't begin to guess.

"In truth, I'm grateful you discovered another door to the human world. Despite the unlikelihood those miserable wretches would ever discover a *Daleth* at such heights, I always prefer to hide them. Just to be safe. One of these days, you must tell me how you discovered it. Was it your dragon senses?"

Doost could easily nod or shake his head if he desired, but he remained stiff and uncommunicative.

She arched a brow at him, shaking her head, but allowed a small smile. "Whatever the case may be, I'm proud of you. Thanks to you, spells have been put in place to prevent anyone from finding it from the human side again. Just make sure not to use it again in the future—you won't be able to find your way back."

Doost's eyes narrowed, and for the first time, he bared his teeth.

"Psh, stop that," she tsked, and smacked him.

My eyes flew wide and I waited for Doost to roast her with his flames.

He did nothing.

"This is for your own good, sweetheart," she said. "I know you don't understand right now, but you will.

I'm looking out for the good of my kingdom." Her kingdom. So she *was* the queen.

Doost snapped his teeth just a handbreadth from her smooth face.

Her red lips curved upward, unconcerned.

"You know you can't hurt me," she said, lifting her perfectly manicured hand to study the gold nails that matched her dress, ignoring those sharp teeth before her. "If I die, you'll never lift the spell. You'd remain a dragon forever. The only way is hearing your true name, darling. You know that better than anyone." She laughed. "Or should I say, you're the *only* one who knows what you need, besides myself."

A spell.

I gasped, then clapped a hand over my mouth.

Doost was under a Jinni spell.

How had I not seen it before?

All this time, he'd been trying to show me, to help me see. That had to be why he'd grabbed me in the first place. He needed to remove the spell.

A spell that could only be lifted with his true name.

This was why he'd brought me here. Whoever he was, this was my clue. And whoever *she* was to *him*, he'd been betrayed by her. I wanted to step out onto the path and make her free him right then and there. The only thing holding me back was the word Doost had scratched in the dirt: *Hide.*

It was dangerous here.

She was dangerous.

He knew that better than anyone.

17

Doost

"*I MISS YOU,*" THE queen said softly.

I snarled at her.

She reached up and stroked my cheek.

Despite the memories returning to me, I let her.

Even closed my eyes.

"I'd turn you back if I could," she whispered. "If only for a few minutes, just to hear your voice again."

I pulled back with a snarl.

Stalked a few feet away.

She smiled sadly. "Even if it meant you would yell at me the whole time, I would do it gladly. But you know I can't risk anyone seeing you. Not yet."

My growls became a roar of rage.

I turned from where Nesrin hid and breathed fire on nearby trees and plants, burning them to ash.

I couldn't help myself.

My roar turned to a groan.

I dropped to the soft grass with a huff.

Lifting her hand, the queen waved toward the remaining flames and they winked out.

Only plumes of smoke left behind.

"Come now." She approached without fear. "You're too old for tantrums."

She placed a hand on my wing.

My lip curled.

But I let her.

"I'm afraid I won't be able to see you for a few short months. Until after the Crowning Ceremony, darling. You know how it is. The servants are beginning to talk about your visit already, and I can't afford any questions right now. On my honor, I promise to bring you home as soon as the ceremony is over."

Home.

The word should've meant something to me, but it was empty.

A swift sadness crossed her face.

She stepped back, signaling for the wolf to follow.

He loped after her.

The scent of him was as familiar to me as if I'd seen his face.

Even so, I couldn't place it.

I followed.

Snarled deep in my throat as they neared Nesrin's hiding place—a clear warning to the wolf not to cross me.

His head tilted to look back. Long face and muzzle dipped in a nod, just barely.

Only a few paces from where Nesrin hid, the queen turned back to face me, misunderstanding. Her gaze dropped to the wolf by her side. "Ah yes, for a moment, I'll allow it."

In the shadows of the trees, which she assumed to be safe from prying eyes, the queen waved a hand over the wolf and he transformed into a Jinni wearing a wolf's pelt.

Barnabas.

His name triggered more memories, jumbled.

I shied back.

He'd been one of my guards and a friend.

He and Gideon.

Barnabas had disappeared from my guard without warning, a few months before…

These thoughts made my head ache.

The tall male glanced at the queen for permission before he strode to meet me.

I leapt to my feet at his approach, ears back.

Was this a trick?

Though my growls were unintelligible, he seemed to understand. "I was coming to warn you when she caught me, my friend. It was either this or banishment."

"Well," the queen drawled from the side, "I can't banish everyone. Someone would start asking questions."

His shoulders stiffened, but he didn't turn around.

I swung my head toward the queen, baring my teeth.

Sighing, she strolled a short distance away.

"She's promised my freedom, same as yours, once this next Crowning Ceremony is complete."

I let out a soft whine, pleading with him.

Just one word would save us both.

"I—" Barnabas choked on emotion, unable to meet my gaze.

His entire demeanor was changed.

Broken.

No longer my bold, confident friend.

"I want to say your name, my prince, I would give anything to say it."

Nesrin gasped from where she hid in the foliage.

Barnabas didn't seem to hear her, glancing over his shoulder at the queen instead, where she waited farther down the path.

He lowered his voice further. "It should be *you* being crowned. I would do anything to make that happen, my prince. But... to my lasting shame, I cannot remember your name. She's taken it from us all."

My animal nature fought for control at his words.

KILL HER. MAKE HER PAY.

Smoke steamed from my nostrils and fire heated in my belly, unbidden, as I narrowed my gaze at her.

HER FAULT.

Leaning down, the queen plucked one of the lavender flowers beside her, snapping the stalk with a sharp twist.

"He's under enchantment to forget your name, I'm afraid," she confirmed, revealing that she'd been eavesdropping still. "Even forget you exist completely, unless someone reminds them. All of Jinn is under that spell. If even one subject recognized you, it would ruin everything, you must understand. And if you persist on going into the human world, I will be forced to do the same to them. Is that clear?"

The fire in my belly died.

I lost the strength to lift my lip or growl.

I lowered my head.

"Come, Barnabas," the queen commanded.

As he obediently returned to her side, he shifted back into wolf form, dropping onto four paws once more.

18

Nes

MY SENSES SCREAMED AT the multiple displays of Jinni magic.

Doost had brought me here for answers, and they danced around the corners of my consciousness, like little fluttering possibilities that I couldn't quite pin down.

My prince? He should be the one being crowned?

None of that reconciled with the enormous beast in front of me. I tucked these details away to consider later.

The queen strolled right past me.

I panicked, pressing deeper into the undergrowth, making myself as small as possible.

Her eyes passed over my hiding place and my heart stopped, but they moved on without a flicker of recognition.

The wolf's nose twitched, but he didn't glance my way either.

"Come home after the Crowning Ceremony is complete," the queen told Doost over her shoulder. "Your people will welcome you with open arms."

With that, she and Barnabas flashed away, leaving behind no trace. There one moment, gone the next.

I blinked, not moving for a long minute, worried she was watching or that she'd reappear as quickly as she'd vanished. When nothing happened, I crawled toward Doost.

I moved to step out of the trees, but he rumbled softly in his chest and shook his head, so slight it was nearly imperceptible.

I stopped.

He dragged his feet along the ground, heading down the trail.

If he wanted me to stay hidden, I wasn't going to argue. I kept beside him, hidden in the foliage along the path, ducking under branches, stepping over roots and plants, and walking around trees, bushes, and ponds until finally we reached the place near the wall where we'd first landed.

Still, I waited until Doost turned to where I hid behind one of the white trees and dipped his sleek head in a nod.

I crept out.

Part of me expected the queen to appear and call her guards, but I ran to Doost without incident, looping dragon skin around his neck as makeshift reins once again, with his help.

"Ready," I gasped as soon as I had a firm grip, and he leapt into the air.

He flew straight up, keeping me out of sight of the castle, but also making me slip down his back until the only reason I stayed on was my death grip on the dragon skin.

I didn't dare scream, but I cried softly, "Please stop, please stop, please stop," until he leveled off.

I let out a gasp of relief.

Vertigo hit me. I closed my eyes to avoid throwing up. My fingers ached from clutching the skin and the ground wouldn't stop spinning, so this time I didn't bother with the view as we flew. I simply lay on his back, eyes closed, gasping shallow breaths.

It felt as if I'd aged a year by the time we began to descend. The landing brought butterflies to my stomach and they scattered when he lurched to a halt and dropped to his belly on the ground.

This time I did fall off.

I rolled down his long wing and the ground rose to hit me in the face. It knocked the air out of me.

Fear made me angry.

As soon as I had enough breath in my lungs, I sat up and yelled, "Never do that again!"

He ignored me.

"Do you hear me? That was terrifying!"

Doost swung his big head around, lowering it to my level and gently nudging my arm in apology. At least, I hoped it was an apology.

I fell back on the grass, exhausted, staring up at the blue sky. "That was… I don't have words for what just happened. That was the queen of Jinn, right?"

Flipping onto my side, I propped my head on my hand so I could see him better as he dipped his chin in a nod. He wasn't meeting my eyes. We hadn't known each other long, but it seemed to me as if he held himself too still, like a statue.

"I knew it," I whispered. I ticked off everything else I'd gathered while hidden. "You're not really a dragon, you're a Jinni. She put some sort of spell on you. And you need to hear your name to break the spell." I jumped up, excited. "So, what is it? I'll say it!"

A distinct groan rumbled from him.

"Well, obviously you can't speak it," I said, crossing my arms. "But you can write. Just spell it out for me."

Doost's head sagged as if he couldn't hold it up anymore, and he shook it, just once.

Understanding dawned and I whispered, "Don't tell me you can't remember either?"

He pulled his tail in, curling into a tight ball, not meeting my eyes anymore.

I struggled to find words. "That seems especially cruel."

Scooting closer until I could reach his tail, I hesitated before awkwardly placing a hand on it. I tried to comfort him. "It's not over yet. There has to be a way I can learn your name..." I trailed off, staring out at the sky and the wildlife surrounding us. "All the Jinni names I've heard are so different from the ones in the human world. Any chance you're named after something in nature?"

His nose twitched. He didn't know.

"What about a creature?"

He heaved his huge shoulder in a shrug.

I sighed in relief. "That's good, because I don't know the names of creatures here anyway."

He snorted at that, and I smiled.

I tried to guess his name all afternoon and into the evening, running through the list of every man in my village as well as the women's names when that didn't pan out.

I wasn't any closer at dusk than I had been when I'd begun.

My stomach rumbled.

* * *

DOOST WAS A PRINCE. Which meant he was rich. No doubt he would handsomely reward the person who helped him break this awful curse. For the first time since my plan to bring home an egg had fallen through, there was a tiny whisper of hope.

I could help him while helping myself.

Even though I might never bring home an egg, if I came back with reward money, I could still rescue my family from debt and return with honor.

The next day, we began our search in earnest.

The Jinni roads weren't dirt like ours were; they were solid and smooth, like a loaf of bread baked by my sister and forgotten in the oven until it was hard as a rock. We followed a quiet road over the hills until a small villa appeared in the distance surrounded on all sides by pools of water.

It was shaped like a set of white boxes with clean angles. "I'll explain first," I told Doost. "You follow once I've prepared them."

Leaving him to his hiding place, I approached the boxy house. Its white walls nearly glowed in the sun. "Hello," I called as I approached. The water around the villa shimmered, clear enough to see the bottom of the pool was made of the same material as the house.

As I drew closer, I frowned.

The water circled the entire home like a moat, but unlike a castle, there wasn't a path to the door.

There was no way to approach at all.

I cleared my throat. "Is someone there?"

The front door of the villa opened and a tall Jinni male stepped out.

Onto the water.

One foot in front of the other, he walked across the surface of the pool as if it were dry land.

"We rarely have human visitors outside the city. What, pray tell, brings you out this way?" he asked softly. The softness wasn't so much like a gentle lamb, but rather a tiger getting ready to pounce.

"I'm here on behalf of the Jinni prince," I began.

"Jinni prince?" He held up a hand, cutting me off. "Human. Do you think me a fool? There is no prince of Jinn." As he said it, he frowned to himself, but after a pause, he turned away, saying, "Go back to your master."

Unless someone reminds them… The queen's words floated back to me.

I opened my mouth to argue, but found it filled with water, as the pool around his home rose over me and swallowed me up.

* * *

I WOKE GASPING FOR breath. The sun directly above turned Doost's head into a silhouette above me.

When he saw me blink, he stepped back so I could sit up.

"What happened?" I croaked, rubbing my throat. A quick glance around me showed the Jinni's home a short distance away, the water around it still and silent, the Jinni nowhere to be seen.

I was soaking wet.

That Jinni had tried to drown me.

"In the name of Jinn," I muttered, trying to shrug off the strange experience. He hadn't even considered the possibility of a prince. The queen's spell was more powerful than I'd expected. "I think it might be better if we ask someone else."

Smoke billowed out of Doost's nostrils, which I'd learned meant he was angry, but he followed me away from the villa with only a few backward glances.

The next time a villa appeared in the distance, I approached with more caution. This one was boxy like the other, but dirt colored, blending in with the forest environment around it.

When I knocked on the front door, the echoes sounded through the house beyond, but no one answered. I tested the doorknob. It was open. Glancing back through the trees, where Doost hid, I shrugged and entered.

The hallway was sleek, cold. I glimpsed a room with low furniture before a voice spoke in front of me.

"How dare you enter my home uninvited?" It was a female voice.

My eyes darted, searching for the owner, without success. "S-sorry, I meant no harm, I'm trying to speak with someone on behalf of... a friend," I finished lamely, remembering the last time I'd brought up the prince of Jinn.

A woman shimmered into existence before me, but only her head.

My eyes grew wide.

"You're human," she said. Her clear blue eyes were hard, narrow.

"I am, but I'd like to help the Jinni—the citizens—the people of Jinn." I stumbled over the unknown etiquette. "They're in danger from the queen."

With a laugh, her whole body appeared, clothed in an elegant lavender dress with laced sandals. "From the queen, you say? I'll be sure to ask her what schemes she's up to at the Crowning Ceremony next month."

"No." I followed her to the door, back outside onto the porch. "No, the Crowning Ceremony will be too late. The prince of Jinn—"

She turned sharply. "What prince?"

"The prince. *The* prince!" I struggled to find words. She cocked her head, considering my words. "I don't know his name, that's why we're here—"

"I've had enough," she said casually, and disappeared.

The lock in the front door snapped shut behind me.

I stood on the porch alone.

Listening intently, I thought I heard her footsteps fading away inside the house, but I couldn't be sure.

So much for that.

* * *

A FEW DAYS OF this passed before I finally admitted it wasn't working. No one would listen. They reacted violently whenever they spied Doost, but they were hardly any better with me.

We needed a new plan.

"We could break into the castle?" I offered one day, after it'd been almost a week.

Doost shook his head violently.

"I won't get caught."

Doost tilted his head meaningfully toward the last villa we'd approached.

"All right. Fair point."

The Jinni there had appeared as a little fawn, nuzzling my hand while I searched the outside of the villa for occupants.

When I'd sat down in frustration to pet him, he'd shifted into a Jinni.

Doost had reared back with a roar, flame pouring out of him.

The shifter barely escaped, turning into a hawk and soaring away on the wind just before the flames reached him.

My skin still felt a bit cooked from proximity.

"Word is going to reach the queen," I muttered. *If it hasn't already.* But I didn't blame him. If I'd been turned into a dragon by a shapeshifter, I'd be wary of them too. "Let's put some distance between us and this place before we ask again."

As we traveled, I studied the tall forest trees with their vivid colors and strangely curving branches and roots. We wouldn't find answers here. An idea struck. "Do you have libraries in Jinn?"

* * *

A JINNI CITY WAS exactly the same and yet nothing like a human city, all at once.

There were buildings in mass, just like back home. Except some of them were floating high above in the clouds. The people—or rather, the Jinn— traveled in and out, assumedly on business. As I tracked a group of them with my eyes, they disappeared. Just... vanished from sight, the way Joram and the queen had done. It was dizzying.

These travelers seemed to be in the minority though. The rest seemed to either not have that ability, or they weren't in the mood to use it.

Still, despite how normal most seemed from a distance, there was something savage about them, as if their extra power made them wary of each other. Many wore armor—which I found especially strange in a culture supposedly so advanced—and some wore furs, though almost none of the pelts were recognizable.

I wasted most of the first day on the outskirts of the city, too anxious to enter, just staring at the sleek buildings, pale streets, and a nearby fountain that had eleven different levels.

If one Jinni at home could drown me, imagine what a few hundred nearby could do to a trespassing human. And Doost couldn't come with me, obviously.

He didn't like that at all.

"It has to be done," I told him, although I was happy to verbalize his side of the argument too. "If they see me and recognize me as a human, they might stop me. They might do a lot worse than that. I know."

We stood at the edge of the trees, where the dirt became packed before turning into a solid, almost marble-like material that spread across the entire city.

"Anyway, I don't see how we have much choice," I muttered to Doost. His heavy pacing vibrated through my feet. It was time to end the one-sided argument before it could last another hour.

I slid my boot onto the solid white material. It didn't seem to sound any alarms at my human presence. "If I don't come back by sundown, you'll know something went wrong," I added, which made him stop pacing to growl.

"Shh, it has to be done." My other foot landed on the strange ground. I was in the city. My heart hammered faster than a wild Dragon Waltz, and I added, "If I don't come back, feel free to tear the city apart looking for me. I won't mind."

He snorted smoke and his tail flicked so wildly that it uprooted a few bushes. This was *his* city, after all.

"I'm only kidding," I tried to reassure him. "If you want to leave the city intact while you rescue me, that's fine."

Another snort, and this time he stalked off into the forest.

"Okay then, good luck to you too." I scowled, but began moving. This side of the city began with long, tall buildings, and I stuck close to the walls, wondering where their version of the Dragon Watch was.

There didn't seem to be any serious guards, besides a few posted by the main road, which seemed ridiculous to me. Although I supposed it made sense. Why would you need to guard against anything if you were the predator?

The signs posted along the buildings in the city were all written in another language.

I hadn't anticipated that.

A surge of frustration made me wish for my climbing tools and a silent day spent finding the next handhold, and the next. At least those were problems I could solve.

This script seemed made up of box shapes, but sometimes one side or another of the box was missing. It was nonsensical. I'd never learn how to read it in a month.

"Human girl," a deep male voice spoke from above me.

I froze, caught standing in the middle of a quiet street. What had given me away? Was it my dark eyes?

Act normal.

I swung around and found myself facing an armored chest with a dark cloak tied over it. I tipped my head back, which unnerved me even more, to meet someone a whole head taller.

This Jinni had deep black hair like Joram, and pale skin, but that was where the similarities ended. His purple eyes were kind, his hair tied back with just a hint of gray in it, and he studied me too closely. "Did your master send you on your own with no instruction?"

Mutely, I nodded.

He sighed, pinching the bridge of his nose. "Did no one explain to you how to navigate the city?"

"I'm—" My voice cracked and I cleared my throat. "I'm looking for the library? But I can't read the signs?" I tried to make them statements, but they turned into questions.

"Ah, yes." His deep voice was strangely soothing. "No one bothers with the old tongue anymore, except when writing. But all the important buildings are in the city center, including the library."

"Thank you," I whispered. Did I bow? Or should I wait for some direction from him?

Fortunately, he swept past me without a backward glance, solving that dilemma. As I moved deeper into the city and it began to be crowded, my eyes caught an occasional blond head or dark skin, and it occurred to me that I might not be the only human here after all.

Still, I kept my guard up.

By the time I found the library, the sun was dangerously close to the horizon.

I scurried out of the city, retracing my steps carefully, remembering my request for Doost to wreck the city on my behalf.

I would come back tomorrow.

* * *

THE LIBRARIANS WEREN'T NEARLY as understanding of a human in their midst as the armored Jinni had been the day before.

The first few days, I hid from them as I searched the shelves that went on throughout endless rooms, but that only seemed to irritate them.

"Stop sniveling," one Jinni said as she shelved books on the upper shelves without touching them. "It only makes them hate you more."

I backed up unconsciously and knocked a book off a shelf behind me. It thumped loudly on the solid floor, echoing across the enormous room, startling a Jinni reading on the other side.

"Stupid humans," he muttered, no doubt aware that his voice carried. "No wonder the queen hates you."

The female Jinni didn't say a word and didn't look at me.

I crept backward, more careful this time. Doost and I needed to move on to a new city, or come up with a new plan; I was drawing too much attention here.

"Is there something specific you're trying to find?" The librarian's cool voice stopped me.

When I glanced back, she was still focused on shelving books.

My mouth was so dry, I had to swallow twice before I could answer. "I hoped to find some history of the throne..." I didn't know if I should say more than that.

She paused, head tilting as she stared into space. "Hmm, a few titles come to mind. What about..." She snapped her fingers multiple times, and with each snap a book appeared in her free hand.

I couldn't speak as she placed the heavy stack of books in my arms, or when she turned back to shelving and moved around the corner to work on the next section.

A shift in the light above was enough to wake me into action. It was just a matter of time. The prince's name had to be written down somewhere within these volumes. I only needed to find it.

Hurrying to an empty corner of the library, I dropped the books onto a table and settled into the chair. Dust flew out of the first book when I opened it. I sneezed. Glancing around for the cranky Jinni, I was grateful to find myself alone this time.

The first tome was leather-bound and thick, with no description on the outside. The title page said *Royalty and Riches: A Study of Jinni Nobility.*

Hours later, I glanced up at the ceiling full of windows to find the sun low in the sky. I slammed the book shut, carrying my stack over to the librarian. "May I check these out?"

"Excuse me?" She stopped what she was working on, turning to face me.

"Uh, can I bring them back another day? I'm not quite finished with them…" Nowhere close to finished. I'd barely begun wading through the first thick volume, and she'd given me four others.

Her forehead wrinkled. "You may not." No further explanation.

"Can I… come back to read them tomorrow?"

She nodded. "As long as they're not needed, you can keep them on the holding shelf in the back."

My gaze followed her finger across the rooms to one filled with windows, sunlight, and shelves. "Thank you." I moved toward it to drop the books off until the next day.

"Just don't tell anyone I'm a sympathizer," she muttered as I walked away. "Because I'm *not*."

* * *

I TRIED AGAIN THE next day.

And the next.

And the next.

Some books were in the old tongue, and I flipped through quickly before moving on. The rest were technically readable, but dense. Muddling through each page was almost as frustrating as listening to Avizun brag about his conquests.

I was able to move through the library undisturbed, as long as I didn't disrupt the peace. Doost and I fell into a routine—sleeping under the stars at night and searching for answers by day.

Each night I offered names to him, on the off chance I might somehow guess his by accident.

"I heard the librarian call someone Abner today. Does that sound familiar?"

Doost paused where he'd been scratching his back against a thick tree. It swayed back into position, leaves falling softly to the forest floor. After we both waited another moment with no results, he snorted smoke and went back to rubbing against the tree. I smiled. He reminded me of a cat. Other days he reminded me of my mother, the way he'd constantly try to feed me. Or pace the forest floor while I was gone. There was a deep rut forming where he'd made a path. If I had to stay in one place and wait to find out if someone was safe, I'd go a little stir-crazy too.

After he fell asleep, I'd lie awake worrying over my family. If Baba had returned from his journey. If he'd been able to pay his debt. If he'd even returned yet at all.

When the month was up, the creditors wouldn't wait any longer. They'd allowed the loans to stretch too long already. This time they would take our home, and if that wasn't enough to cover the debt, they'd take my family too.

I bathed in cold streams most days, eating the food Doost brought me, and continued to search through books for an answer.

As I read, I began to suspect something, but wasn't sure how to prove it. It seemed to me that a Jinni prince should be mentioned frequently in texts about the royalty. Even just once. But there was only ever a mention of a Jinni princess.

Sometimes the complete lack of Doost as a Jinni made me question my own sanity. Had I made this entire thing up? No, I'd heard the queen clearly.

Certain passages discussing recent family members seemed to almost have information missing, as if the spell had erased every hint of him. One day I found a line where I felt certain Doost's true name *should* be:

The royal family received five of the highest quality horses from the human lands, a kingdom known as Sagh, ruled by King Amir.   He prized the stallion.   The queen gave one to him.

Either the author had been drinking while writing, or there were large chunks missing.

I sighed, replacing the books at the end of the day yet again.

Time was running out, and I was beginning to think my efforts to help Doost were as useless as my efforts to bring home an egg had been.

* * *

ONE NIGHT, AFTER COUNTING how many moons had passed since I'd left home, I got up to pace, unable to sleep.

I'd been gone nearly a full month.

In the dark, I strode back and forth on a hillside a short distance away. Doost's heavy footsteps made me turn to face him. He yawned, sitting back on his haunches and blinking at me sleepily.

"Sorry if I woke you," I mumbled, continuing to pace. "I couldn't sleep."

He blinked at me.

When I didn't say anything further, he waited until I paced toward him to lower his head and nudge my arm. My whole side really.

I had to uncross my arms to catch my balance or risk tipping over. I half smiled, but it faded quickly.

"It's my family," I found myself sharing. I'd told him bits and pieces about them over the last few weeks, but nothing about my father's trip or our debt. At first because I didn't trust him, then later, I'd wanted to wait until his spell was broken. I had thought that when he asked how he could ever repay me for saving him, I'd share my story.

He waited, blinking patiently.

Once I started to explain, it all poured out. All the debt accumulated over the years. The way my mother and siblings only added to it. Even my father in his attempts to make things better. "I thought I could save them, but I failed."

A pause, then a questioning nudge.

I sighed, dropping to sit on the ground, weary at the memory. "Remember when you first found me? When I was climbing the cliffs?" I knew he did. "I was looking for a dragon's egg."

It sounded ridiculous when I said it out loud, but I made myself explain. "I thought if I could find something so rare and beautiful, it would fetch a price that could cover our debt and then some. They wouldn't be able to bother us anymore. If they take our home, my family won't survive. Worse, they might make my family pay the debt with their lives. Roohstam would be horribly lazy and earn beatings. Zareen would suffer terribly under the pressure. And Shadi…" I shook my head with a humorless laugh. "She would terrify them. But in the end, they would break her too."

A tear escaped. I hadn't meant to get emotional. Before I could wipe it away, his soft nose pressed against my cheek and caught it.

I sniffed, not sure why I felt embarrassed. "I just wanted to save my family. I think I knew it was stupid." I scoffed at myself. "I thought I could somehow find and carry an egg home. Without getting eaten. Pretty foolish, huh?" I sighed, lying down in the soft grass and staring at the Jinni constellations, which had begun to feel as familiar as my bedroom ceiling back home. He curled up next to me. "When I saw how big the eggs were, it ruined everything. Years of hard work, Doost, *years* of learning to climb! And all along it never would've worked. I know that now."

For a minute, we sat in silence. I scratched absently at the dragon-skin vest I still wore, which had become almost part of me, before I murmured, "I bet this skin would've fetched a good price."

Rolling onto my side, I propped my head on my hand to look at him. "You're a good listener, you know that?" I smiled at him, trying to lighten the mood. "Anyway," I rolled back with a sigh, "as much as I want to go back home and help, there's nothing I can do."

He was still. Thoughtful. His eyes were no longer sleepy, but I couldn't tell what he was thinking. Maybe it didn't matter.

The stars twinkled above, an ever-present reminder of just how far from home I truly was. I lay there, unable to stop thinking about my family and what might be happening. *Has my father returned from the Shah's Council yet? Has his plan succeeded?* Questions hounded me. It was nearly dawn before slccp finally camc.

* * *

THE NEXT DAY, DOOST broke our routine.

Instead of wandering the forest while I visited the city, he turned in a new direction, which led to a full day of walking. Only on the second morning did I realize he'd taken a direct path back toward the original cave where the word 'stay' was still scratched into the wall. *Is this an accident?* With Doost leading, it was hard to tell.

I hadn't entered the caves since the day my fever had broken. My arm was fully healed now, except for thick scars from the claw marks. "What're we doing here?"

He lowered his big head to my level, reassuring, before heading into the tunnel. Inside the entrance, he paused, waiting.

"The queen said if you went through the portal, you wouldn't be able to come back," I reminded him. "She meant the caves, right?"

Doost only blinked at me.

"Are you sure you want to leave here? I know she said she would turn you back into a Jinni, but what if she decides it's too far and doesn't want to come find you? I—" I couldn't believe I was arguing against going home. "I don't want to be the reason you're stuck in the human world."

He only swung his head around and began to move forward.

I sucked in a breath, blew out my cheeks, and sighed. "Fine." Walking up to him, I placed a hand on his side. "Lead the way."

As it grew too dark to see, I leaned into him more and more. That sickly sweet smell filled my nostrils and coated my tongue until I felt like it permeated my pores. He took us through the winding tunnels at a snail's pace for my benefit.

When we reached the pit that I'd stumbled into the first time through, he warned me with a low growl, and lit up the caves with a small fire. With the echo of flames still burned into my eyes, we circled the pit with care, and continued on.

Finally, I caught a glimmer of sunlight from the other side. My heart did a little somersault in my chest and the ache made me realize just how much I'd missed the human world.

Once inside the familiar cave where I'd first arrived, I let my hand slip from his side. The cool air where his warm scales had been made me feel oddly alone. The rib cage sat where it had always been, but somehow looked smaller now, reminding me of how I'd huddled inside it in terror. So much had happened over the last few weeks. I didn't feel like the same person.

It was only an hour past dawn, but it was as if we'd turned back time to when I'd first arrived here.

Doost stomped his foot on the rock floor the way we'd grown accustomed to when he was asking me to stay behind.

"Why?" I frowned. But of course, he couldn't answer.

I sighed and nodded.

He launched himself from the mouth of the cave into the sky and flew off on an unseen current.

Stepping up to the edge, I knelt to peer down below. As I'd remembered, it was impossible to free-climb, far too smooth. The clouds blocked my view of the ground completely, creating a strange sensation of an entirely new ground made up of white fluff that played tricks on my mind, begging me to step out onto it.

Instead, I stretched out to lie on my stomach, chin resting on top of my hands, gazing out at the white abyss below and blue skies above. I missed home. I'd told myself I wouldn't complain to Doost anymore, but being this close drew up all the feelings I'd been pressing down for weeks. *Is my family okay? Has my father come home?*

Doost was gone for hours. I had to crawl into the back of the cave to avoid any departing dragons spotting me, having watched over a dozen fly out from their hollows in the cliff wall.

It was nearly noon when he returned, without warning, as if he'd flown up from below. He held something in his front claws. At first I couldn't make out what he carried, but as he carefully set it down on the ground in front of us, I stepped forward to join him and my lips parted in amazement.

It was a dragon's egg.

19

Nes

UNLIKE THE EGG I'D found before, this one was smaller, as wide as a dinner plate at the bottom and tapering to the size of my fist near the top. Much more manageable. It was a stunning orange-gold color, which made me wonder if the egg's color reflected the dragon inside.

He did this for me? I came closer, kneeling in front of the egg and tilting my head to look at him.

He averted his eyes, almost shyly.

"Does this mean…?" My heart fluttered, but I shoved the feeling down; my hope would be his defeat. "You're letting me go? Don't tell me you're giving up on breaking your curse?"

He dipped his head in a nod, and left it low, not meeting my eye. Pulling away to face the tunnel, he presented me with his back.

"I can come back in a few days," I found myself offering. He shifted slightly, but otherwise didn't move. "I swear! After I bring my family the egg and help my father pay back his debt, I can research names and write a whole list to try!" I circled around him to see his face.

His head hung low and he wouldn't meet my eyes.

"Doost." I smiled as I said it.

Usually the nickname I'd given him cheered him up. Not today. He didn't respond.

I hesitated, not usually comfortable touching him, but I dared to reach out to his long face and pressed a hand under his chin. He allowed me to lift it—I'd never have the strength on my own—and his yellow eyes met mine.

"I don't know how much time you have left," I murmured. The queen had said a few short months, but how long was that exactly? How much of that time had we already used? I cleared my throat and continued, "But there's still a chance we can figure out your true name." I held his head in both hands, trying to show my sincerity. "I swear to you, in the name of Jinn, that I will come back."

The smallest spark of hope lit his eyes. His head grew lighter in my hands, though he didn't pull away. Instead, he leaned in, closing the space between us, and gently rested his head against my arm and shoulder. I paused, surprised. We'd only touched for warmth or when helping each other. But my arms moved as if they had a will of their own, wrapping around his head. I stroked his ear, which was soft as a feather, and leaned into him. We stayed that way until I stepped back.

"We should go," I said finally, feeling guilty.

I still had my bag, ragged and worn, but otherwise in good shape. Pulling it off my shoulders, I set it down and placed the golden egg inside. I'd expected the egg to be fragile, but the shell felt as tough as Doost's scales and the smelly old skin I still wore. It was warm and heavy.

Tying the bag shut carefully, I paused before lifting it to glance at him again. Sometime in the last month, I'd come to care for him. He was more a friend to me than anyone back home.

"Give me two days," I told him. "I'll find a buyer and bring the money to my family—let them know I'm okay. That'll give me time to… explain what happened." We both knew that was false. There was no way any normal family would understand their daughter leaving them to return to a dragon. I left it unsaid that I didn't plan to tell them that part. As far as they were concerned, I'd left nearly a month prior to find a dragon's egg and I was coming home with one. That's all they ever needed to know.

I hefted the bag with the egg inside. It weighed as much as the neighbor's small dog back home. Though it didn't seem fragile, I still moved with care as I shifted it onto my back, pulling the straps tight so it wouldn't fall off. It was heavy enough to make me feel slightly off balance.

"We can meet at the base of the cliffs where we first met." I tried to smile, but it wobbled. "I'm not climbing all the way up here for you. Even if I had twice as many ropes as my first climb, I'm horribly out of shape." I flexed. "See?"

That earned me one of his toothy grins and I smiled back until he lowered himself to the ground and stretched out his wing for me to mount.

Heart pumping faster as I anticipated the flight, I hoisted my bag with the egg inside and carefully stepped onto that curve where his shoulder met his wing.

Climbing onto his back, I straddled his neck and used the dragon-skin vest as a makeshift harness, the way I had on our last flight. "I hate this so much," I mumbled as I held on to the skin and let him take the other end in his teeth, bringing it around until I could grasp it. "Give me a moment... I need to mentally prepare." He stayed as still as a statue, waiting. "Okay." I inhaled deeply and blew it out. "Let's go."

As he stood, I slid backward and then lurched forward, already losing my seat. "Let's make a deal," I said, trying to make light of my fears to avoid an outright panic attack. "If I fall off, do you swear you'll catch me?"

His neck curved and his big head swung around to bump me gently on the arm.

"I'm not worried," I protested. "I'm not."

I recognized the soft growl as his version of a chuckle. "Fine, I'm terrified. Happy? Let's get this over with."

He ambled over to the mouth of the cave where the open sky faced us. I tried to move with his rhythm, the way I would with a horse, but his gait was so heavy that each step threw me sideways. I hunkered down, stretching across his back, holding on to my makeshift reins as tight as possible, and closed my eyes as we reached the edge. I was having trouble breathing. My chest was tight and my head was fuzzy.

His footsteps swung me one way, then the other, followed by a terrifying drop that left my stomach somewhere above us. I couldn't breathe until we leveled out and it was easier to hold my seat. I could tell he was extremely careful to stay level for me. Still, I kept my eyes squeezed shut. No need to make things worse.

But shortly after we took flight, he growled, growing louder when I didn't respond right away.

"What?" I groaned, peeking out of one eye, trying not to notice the way the ground flew past so far below. We were as high as the clouds, blending in—I hoped—so the humans wouldn't see us, but through the haze in the distance were a few towns interspersed among the trees. The orange rooftops made the tiny cities pop between the green forests and open plains, and from this distance, people were almost invisible, just little specks moving about.

The closest one was Heechi.

* * *

I FINALLY UNDERSTOOD HIM after he circled the towns the second time. He didn't know which one to aim for.

"Go left," I made myself speak over the nausea. "Heechi is the town farthest from the Srosh castle. But set me down a few miles out in the woods," I added. Each town had a constant Dragon Watch and the sun was directly overhead, making it impossible to hide. If we flew too close, the bells would ring and they would begin trying to shoot Doost out of the sky.

A fierce dragon might not think much of them from a distance, but their aim was wickedly good.

He flew on and I raised my voice. "Here. Set me down here. Don't go any closer."

Doost swung his head to the side to glance at me in clear disagreement.

"I don't want them to see you," I said. "Just trust me. Please. Land here."

His answering growl vibrated through me, and he obeyed, dipping toward the ground at a speed that made my stomach feel as light and airy as a spinning top.

It was closer to town than I'd like, but hopefully no one had seen, and still a good hour's walk, if not more.

He landed lightly and I slipped off his back immediately, not bothering to hide my relief. "Thank you. I've never seen such a beautiful valley. And what luscious grass. Let's stay on the ground and never do that again. In fact," I patted the bag on my back, "now that I have the egg, I don't think I'll ever have a taste for heights again."

I caught myself, but not fast enough, and I tried to fix my mistake at the hurt look in his eye. "That is— except for when I return to help you. Obviously." I meant it. I *would* come back.

"Want to walk with me?" I offered to avoid the goodbye a bit longer. "It'll be safe on the ground. At least for a bit."

We set off and I didn't speak much, other than to point out how much farther we had. Doost, already hard to understand to begin with, reduced his responses to an occasional growl, and after a while, not even that.

When the road into town appeared a short distance ahead, I knew we'd come far enough. "Well..." I stopped and turned to face him. "This is where I leave you. But I promise, Doost," I met his gaze and held it. "I swear to you I will come back. Two days from now. At the bottom of the cliffs."

His eyes stayed on the ground beside me.

What could I give to him to make him believe me? I had nothing. Only words.

My hand stretched toward him. Hesitating, I stopped just before I touched him. I chewed on my lip. All the dragons that had attacked our village over the last few decades ran through my mind. This went against everything I'd ever known.

Swallowing the thought, I let one hand rest against his warm, scaly cheek and placed the other over my heart. "I swear to you on my life and honor. I will return."

His soft nose snuffled. He closed his eyes and leaned into my palm with a soft sigh. I didn't know if he believed me or not, but I would prove it.

I turned to go, but stopped and pivoted to face him one final time. "Don't fly from here, okay? Make sure you walk back to where we landed. And more importantly, wait until dark."

He snorted at that.

"Please," I said, walking backward toward the road. "For me? I don't want to worry about you."

That softened his features and he settled back on his haunches to watch me go.

I turned away and walked to the road telling myself I wouldn't look back, but when I reached the dirt road, I did, just once.

He was still where I'd left him.

Watching.

20

Doost

I'D KNOWN FOR WEEKS now: she was my last hope.

And still, I'd walked through that tunnel. Flown on the current to the nearest nest, stolen an egg, and given her permission to leave me.

Her dark eyes had lit. A sheen of tears. And I could only be thankful for the lack of expression in my beastly form.

My head had lowered as she examined the egg.

Conflicting desires had raged. Bring her to her home, or snarl at her and chase her back into Jinn.

I'd pushed that base urge away.

There was no going back to Jinn.

My mother had made sure of that.

I'd remembered everything.

I didn't need to wander the caves to know they would never lead back to my homeland.

No going back.

Now, the forest surrounded me. The dirt road wove this way and that, letting me glimpse her back twice more, before she was gone for good.

Not gone for good. She'd promised to come back.

My wings brushed the ground, somehow too heavy to bother holding up anymore. Promises weren't to be trusted.

No one could be trusted.

I sank deep into melancholy, moving just far enough into the woods to be out of sight of the road, before lying down and curling my head and tail around my body.

If only I could see her from the skies. It would ease my worries that she'd lied.

A growl rumbled through me.

She had not *lied.*

Smoke rolled from my nostrils. I shifted, unable to get comfortable, but I didn't get up. I couldn't find it in myself to begin traveling yet. To reach our meeting place, to wait, to be disappointed.

Everyone lied.

My entire life in Jinn was a foundation of lies.

Even my own mother lied.

My only true confidants had been my sister, who had disappeared decades ago, and my two closest friends, who I'd hoped would search for me. But Barnabas was lost, and it seemed Gideon had abandoned me.

Why should Nesrin be any different?

If only I could fly over her little town and see her. Just one look from the skies could ease my mind.

No.

I flung out my tail in frustration. It smashed into the base of a thick tree, cutting it in half. Sharp bits flew in all directions as the top half of the tree came crashing down and landed with a boom.

My tail was unharmed, of course. The scales guarded me. If only I could grow scales over my heart.

21

Nes

I STRODE INTO TOWN feeling like a complete stranger, as if I'd been gone years instead of just under a month. Covered in dirt and grime from only occasionally bathing in streams, I was embarrassed, but it wasn't my filthy appearance that drew everyone's attention. Their eyes caught on the dark green scales of my dragon-skin vest glittering in the heavy afternoon sunlight, before fastening on the scars across my arm. Whispers flew.

No one welcomed me back, which I took to mean my family had hidden my disappearance from small-town gossip. That was about to change.

"What day is it?" I asked the blacksmith as he passed in the other direction.

When he told me, I breathed a sigh of relief. I'd come home just in time. Two days before the creditors were to call.

I knew exactly what I needed to do.

I stopped the children running through the streets by taking their ball. Once their eyes lifted from my vest and scars to my face, I infused excitement into my voice. "Spread the word. This afternoon, a dragon's egg is going to be auctioned to the highest bidder in the marketplace!"

Their eyes grew wide as saucers and they took off, forgetting their ball in their haste.

"Make sure you send someone to the Shah family," I called after them. They lived an hour's distance from Heechi, close enough to attempt governing, but far enough from the Dragon Cliffs that seeing a dragon was a novelty. It would be cutting it close, but there should be enough time if a messenger left now for them to reach the auction in time.

My next stop was their mothers and the other gossips lingering in the market stalls.

"What happened to your arm?" one woman asked. I ignored them.

The hunters had heard the news too. "Good luck trying to sell that skin today. Haven't you heard? Someone's got an egg to sell."

"Probably just a replica," one of the men on Dragon Watch called down from the tower, joining the conversation.

Just like that, they were in a yelling match, and I was forgotten.

The whole town was gathering near the auctioneer stand, hollering to each other across the spaces to ask if anyone had more news on the mysterious egg.

I hoped that if a member of the Shah family didn't show, at least a noble or two from nearby cities might hear the rumors in time.

The weight of the egg on my back made me keep to the edges of the crowd, but not one of them gave me a second glance. For once, I was glad.

A peek at the sun told me I still had another hour. Slipping away, I started asking a few familiar faces if they'd seen my father come home. *No. No, I haven't seen him.* I desperately wanted to go home and find out for myself, but I couldn't face my family until this was done.

Continuing to ask around, I grew more and more anxious as the answer stayed the same, until a man from the Dragon Watch spoke up. "I saw him slip through the gate yesterday evening. He didn't speak to anyone, didn't look like he wanted anyone to know he was back."

"Did he look well? Did he go to the creditors?"

"His clothes were dirty, like he'd been sleeping on the ground..." The man trailed off, studying me. "I don't mean any disrespect, but wherever he went, it didn't look like it went well for him. He hasn't come into town since he returned."

Thanking him, I turned away, shoulders hunched. That didn't sound like a man returning from a successful business trip. More like a return in disgrace.

There was one other visit I needed to make, for Doost's sake. I made my way to Maadar Bozorgi's small home on the edge of Heechi. The streets were quiet on this side of town.

When I knocked, Bozorgi's frail voice called for me to enter.

"I was wondering if you'd ever come back to visit." She grinned, mostly gums, at the sight of me, waving me in. "I've just made tea, help yourself."

To be polite, I poured a cup. "Sorry, I've been… busy."

She *tsked* at my excuse, and my cheeks warmed, but I didn't explain. Not yet.

Setting my bag and its precious cargo ever so carefully on the floor beside the low table, I sat across from Bozorgi and warmed my hands on the cup, too nervous to drink. The impending auction loomed over me. *What if it isn't enough to save my family?* My original reason for coming here escaped me as I stared at the wooden design over the window that caused the light falling inside to swirl in beautiful patterns on the rugs.

"You forget my age, *dokhtari*." Bozorgi winked as she finished her own tea. "If you don't ask whatever plagues you now, you might never get a chance."

I tried to smile at her teasing, but instead cleared my throat, catching my leg bouncing anxiously. With a deep breath, I dove straight to the heart of it. "Maadar, do you remember the name of the prince of Jinn?"

She clucked, staring into her empty cup as if the answer was there. "The prince of Jinn, mmm? You know our people and the Jinn have never really gotten along."

I held back a sigh, pressing my lips together. I wasn't in the mood for one of her usual history lessons. "So you've said."

"They cursed us years ago," she continued, as if I hadn't spoken. "Our proud tribes, once their equal, have forgotten who we are. What we can do."

Once I would have dismissed her ramblings outright, but after spending most of the last month in Jinn, I paused. Glancing at the window, I marked the angle of the sun. There wasn't time for this. *I'll come back later,* I promised myself. "I'm sorry, Maadar, I have to go. Thank you for the tea." I took it to her small sink and picked up my bag.

"Young people. Always in such a hurry." She chuckled as I opened the door. "I thought you wanted to know the name of the prince?"

One foot already in the street, I swung around to face her. "You know it?"

"Of course." She shuffled over to the sink to wash the cups. "You should always keep an eye on your enemy."

With her back to me, I let my head fall back and closed my eyes, struggling to keep my voice patient as I asked, "What is it?"

"Malakai."

My nose crinkled at the ridiculous sounding name. "Are you certain?"

"As certain as I am that the Heechi tribes are the ancestors of the dragons."

My heart sank. She'd spouted this idea for years and was the laughingstock of town. *She's still convinced fairy tales are true. No doubt she's created this name for him in her mind as well.* My last attempt to learn Doost's true name was yet another failure.

"Thank you, Maadar," I mumbled as I shut the door behind me, trudging back through the streets toward town. I could only hope this wasn't an omen for how the auction was about to go.

The audience had grown to ten times the size I'd expected. Many wealthy families stood amidst the townspeople, but I didn't see any sign of the Shah family of Srosh, not even the Shah's son, who was a renowned dragon fanatic. I'd hoped, optimistically I suppose, that he'd have heard news of the auction in time. And though I scanned the crowd twice, my family was nowhere to be found either. My father's shame must've been great if my family would miss the chance to see an egg.

With only a few hours left until sunset, I climbed onto the small platform in the middle of the town square that was usually used for auctions and the rare storyteller or speaker traveling through town. I should've hired an auctioneer to handle this next part. My heart pumped wildly with nerves.

"What're you doing?" someone jeered. "Get off the stage."

"I'll give you ten chickens for the skin," another called. It was insultingly low, even if I had been there to barter the dragon skin.

"We're not here for the skin," Avizun shouted over them. "We're here for the egg! Get off the stage, girl." His fellow hunters cheered in agreement.

Without a word, I swung my bag down, setting it carefully on the ground as people milled about in front of me.

I grinned, nerves vanishing, as I placed my hands inside the bag and drew out the symbol of my family's freedom. I lifted the egg above my head proudly. Proof that everything they'd said about me was wrong. Though, in many ways, they'd been far more right about my odds than I'd have liked to admit; they'd never know just how close I'd come to failing.

The egg glowed in the light of the late afternoon sun, making it look as if it were truly made of gold. A brief hush blanketed the crowd before the clamor of thinly-veiled gossip grew twice as loud. Their gasps were worth every minute of pain and exhaustion. I savored the awe and delight on their faces, letting them take it in.

"Where did you get that?" Avizun's booming voice again rose above the rest. "Were you playing in the mud and decided to create a fake?"

Anger burned hot. Even now I wasn't good enough for them.

Almost as one, they drew closer, packing in to get a closer look, calling out to each other, debating whether or not the egg was a fake, until it was so loud I could hardly hear myself think.

I gently lowered the egg to the auctioneer's high podium, setting it on display and using my bag to keep it stable and upright.

Maadar Bozorgi's words came back to me. *If you know the truth, their untruths will roll off you.*

No one was going to take this victory from me.

This egg was mine.

I was not cursed, and however the egg came to me, I was the first to ever return with one.

I flung up a hand to silence them. Only when they obeyed did I reply. "It is authentic. From the Dragon Cliffs." The late afternoon sun worked in my favor, as I'd hoped it would; its rays shone through the thin shell and the barest silhouette was visible within. In the awed silence, I shouted the words I'd only ever dreamed of saying. "To the highest bidder!"

It was as if I'd set off a race and the bids were the runners, scrambling madly over each other, each trying to be in first place, instantly raising the price to a shocking number.

I kept still, barely blinking.

When it passed the price I'd imagined and showed no signs of stopping, I clenched my jaw and schooled my face to complete disinterest. It was difficult.

When the number doubled, then tripled, I lost the ability to swallow, but still I stood tall, pretending confidence.

Out in the crowd a voice carried over the rest in a tone that made others turn to look. "I'll double that price and pay you now."

I recognized his proud swagger and that red cloak immediately. The gold crown twisting across his brow confirmed it.

It was the Shah's son.

In normal circumstances, he would never venture so near the Dragon Cliffs. Only the Heechi citizens and surrounding tribes braved the proximity.

But word of the egg had reached him in time, just as I'd hoped it would.

Openmouthed, I snapped my teeth together and nodded. "Agreed." I was blinking too much, but I couldn't help myself. This was everything I'd hoped for and more.

The crowd parted as he strode forward, a contingent of a dozen guards following, forcing the citizens of Heechi to step back.

Before everyone, the Shah's guards set down a heavy treasure chest and opened the lid, revealing it to be filled to the brim with gold and jewels. "Is this acceptable?" the son asked with smirk.

Momentarily at a loss for words, I could only nod.

He waved for his men to close the lid and stepped toward the dragon's egg, where it still rested on the podium. He touched the golden side reverently. *I wonder what he'll do with it.* A hushed silence fell, different than before, as no doubt everyone else wondered the same thing. Would the hatchling live in captivity? And would the Shah's son tame it if it did? Or maybe use it for sport or for something else altogether?

When he lifted the egg, cradling it like a new babe as he set it within a large velvet-lined box, it woke me from my trance.

"I'll need your men to deliver the payment to my estate," I declared with more confidence than I felt. No sense getting robbed before I even made it home. With some bargaining on their fee, the prince agreed to send four men, and we shook on it.

When I lifted my empty bag, my arms felt oddly light and free. The remaining guards lifted the treasure between the four of them.

Since they didn't know where I lived, I took the long way that would pass the credit house without any protest from them.

The crowd began to disperse, but some of the more curious stayed with us, wanting to see what I would do with all my new wealth.

It was oddly reassuring. No one would risk stealing from me with the entire town watching.

I strode up to the creditors building, with the Shah's men holding the treasure chest on my heels, and banged on the metal door knocker until someone appeared.

When the door swung open, I demanded an audience with the owner of the establishment.

We passed one of the burly men who'd made a visit to my father a month earlier, but I pretended not to recognize him.

I was led into the owner's office, while the Shah's men waited outside.

The chief creditor was as thick and muscled as his guards, with a shrewd look in his dark eyes.

"I've come to settle my father's debt," I told him. "Every coin owed to you by the Ahmadi family. And don't try to deceive me," I cautioned before he could reply. "I know exactly how much he owes you."

The big man moved to sit in his chair, waving across his desk for me to take the seat opposite him.

I remained standing.

"Well, we have to consider interest."

"I know the interest," I interrupted. "It was listed in detail in the letter last month, along with the due date."

"I see." He folded his hands and considered me. "Then all we will need is some time to count it and—"

"Perfect," I said, pulling the wooden chair out and letting it screech across the floor to emphasize my interruption. "We'll count it now."

Though he tried to draw it out, the Shah's men and I left the credit house an hour later, as the sun dipped toward the horizon, with a much lighter chest of gold and an equally lighter step. In my hand, I held the note of agreement of a debt paid in full.

There were a few stragglers from the crowd lingering outside. I spoke loudly for anyone listening. "These four men bore witness today to a debt paid in full." Some additional insurance, just in case they thought me a simple girl who could be ignored later. Without a doubt, the whole town would know what the gold from the egg had purchased by the next morning.

It was time to go home.

I found myself nervous, now that it was time. Brushing the dirty strands of dark hair behind my ears, I took a minute to rebraid it. After contemplating my ragged ensemble, I tugged off the dragon skin that had become like my own skin, rolling it up and placing it in my nearly empty bag. Hopefully I looked more like myself now, in my usual climbing gear of loose pants, shirt, and boots. There was nothing I could do about the smell.

"This way." I gestured for the Shah's men to follow and they shadowed me the rest of the way home without complaint.

At the front gate, I stopped. "You can leave it here."

"We'll bring it inside for you," the closest guard replied, and the others nodded.

I smiled my thanks, too overwhelmed to trust my voice.

I was nearly home.

It took forever for someone to answer the gate. My siblings still acted as if we had a myriad of servants, so I wasn't surprised when the figure approaching turned out to be the cook. When she recognized me through the iron bars of the gate, she picked up her skirts and ran.

"Nesrin!" she cried, unbarring the gate and swinging it wide for us. "You're alive!"

I grinned, hugging her, letting her wipe her tears and run screaming into the house for my family to come.

Leading the men inside, I gestured toward the inner courtyard wall for them to leave the payment there, thanking them.

My sisters arrived as they left, screeching at the top of their lungs, nearly breaking my body with the strength of their hugs. My brother joined them, everyone talking at once. My mother stepped up to us with tears streaming down her face and I thought she might yell, but instead she crushed me to her chest and sobbed.

I began to worry that my father was in worse shape than the Dragon Watch guard had let on, when he hobbled through the door.

I stepped away from my mother and my siblings to hold out the piece of paper I'd kept safe during it all. "This is for you, Baba." I bit my lip as he took it, forcing myself to wait while he read.

"How did you—?" The paper shook in his hands.

"I found an egg, Baba." I grinned, wanting him to be proud of me.

His eyes caught on my scars. "What in the name of Jinn happened to your arm?"

I swallowed but forced my voice to be light. "Part of the hunt. It's a long story."

"Long story," he mumbled and frowned. "Your mother was worried you'd been injured or worse! If I'd been home, I'd never—"

"I know," I interrupted. "I'm sorry, Baba."

"*Never* do that again, do you understand?" His voice cracked.

My siblings shifted uncomfortably. The cook slipped out to give us privacy while my mother wept openly.

I ducked my head, tears filling my eyes. "Yes, Baba."

"All that matters now is you're alive," he said, dropping the paper and stepping forward to wrap his arms around me. He began to weep as well. "I'm so, so terribly proud of you, my little dragon hunter." For once, the nickname made me smile.

* * *

NOT EVEN HALF A day had passed since I'd left Doost behind, but already the memory of my last month felt distant, as if I'd dreamt it. The moment I pointed to the chest of gold in the corner, my family flew to it, digging through the enormous amount of gold and jewels left over, exclaiming all the things they would buy.

"We'll be the center of every feast and dance for years to come!" Shadi declared joyously.

"I can buy that maroon gown in the store window that I wanted so desperately," Zareen added on a blissful sigh.

"Nice job, little sister." Roohstam grinned and slapped me on the back. "I always knew you would find an egg."

I rolled my eyes at the blatant lie, but grinned back at him. Everything was falling into place. A twinge of sadness surprised me.

My mother hugged me again, but this time she pulled back, nose wrinkling, and ordered me to take a bath.

I heated water over the fire and took a long soak in the tub. After the last month of bathing in cold streams, the warmth was exquisite. Scrubbing at my skin with soap, I cleaned the dirt out of my pores and for the first time in a long while, I finally felt clean.

As I made my way back downstairs in a simple tunic, leggings, and boots, I stopped at the doorway, watching my family whip themselves into a frenzy over the gold and jewels.

I tried to imagine what Doost might be doing right now. Whether walking or waiting, I could only hope he'd stay on the ground until nightfall like I'd asked.

Only a bit longer before it'd be safe. I stepped up to the window to find the sun touching the horizon.

Biting my lip, I slipped outside. I wanted to see him, but even more, I hoped I didn't. That would be safer.

I didn't notice Baba at first when he slipped outside to join me. He studied the dusky sky with me, keeping the silence for a bit. The light blues slowly deepened. Nightfall couldn't come fast enough.

In the end, I was the one to break the silence. "How was your trip?"

He didn't answer at first. "It was… nowhere near as profitable as yours."

I peeked at him out of the corner of my eye; the shadows on his face deepened the dark circles under his eyes.

"And it was terribly long," he added.

"What happened to the Jinni with you?" I asked after a long pause. "I thought with his travel, the trip was only supposed to take a few days?"

He sighed, rubbing a tired hand across his face as he spoke, "The Shah's Council liked my idea for bringing value back to the crops with Jinni magic. So much, in fact, that they hired Joram to work for them instead. He left me to find my own way home."

So his plan had fallen through just like I'd thought it would. That didn't bring me any comfort. I wanted to ask why he'd hired Joram in the first place, or why he'd revealed his full plan to the council before striking a deal. It was so typical. But thinking that way wouldn't help either of us.

Before I could find the right words, swallowing what felt like a jagged rock in my throat, he revealed a small flower I'd not noticed him holding.

"There is one bit of good news." His smile was more pained than it used to be as he held out a white rose, with sparkling silver along the tips of each petal.

The familiar tingle of Jinni magic that kept it alive and fresh, permanently blooming, whispered across my skin.

I accepted it. The magic warmed to me and the rose let off a sweet scent that carried a feeling of contentment. "How?"

"Before the council met, Joram and I were kept waiting outside and when I found the Jinni rose bush, I thought to myself, 'This will be perfect for my sweet Nesrin. It can be the first of many gifts I'll bring home.'"

His face darkened, and I knew there was more.

"Tell me."

"They said anyone who stole from the Shah's Council could not be trusted. It was the perfect excuse for them to give the contract to another."

"But it was just a rose!" I snapped. "That's hardly stealing!"

He dipped his head, as much agreement with traitorous thinking as he would allow himself. "I returned to town only last night, and was preparing to turn myself in to the creditors. To beg them to take me and leave you, your mother, and your siblings in peace." His solemn gaze trapped me in place, and when I didn't look up, he took my shoulders, turning me to face him. "Daughter, it is because of you that our family is whole."

His words brought tears to my eyes. They filled my throat until it was impossible to swallow. I dipped my chin in a nod and hugged him.

After a moment, he stepped back and a smile returned to his face. "Fortunately for me, I have a daughter with business sense that far exceeds my own. I look forward to hearing her tale."

I felt his eyes on me then, waiting for me to spill my secrets. I let the corner of my mouth lift in a smile, but didn't meet his eyes.

There was no explanation he would understand.

A chaotic throng broke the peaceful silence as my siblings poured out of the house, arguing over nonsense.

Zareen kissed my cheek as they joined us, before whirling away to show us the newest dance they were doing these days. Such spectacular affairs, which they would now be invited to attend once more, because of me.

Shadi joined the dancing, making Roohstam be her partner. They called for me to join them.

I shook my head, but smiled.

"What is that?" Baba's voice immediately brought everything into sharp focus.

I ripped my gaze from the dancing, shading my eyes, terrified of what I might find. "No," I whispered, covering my mouth in horror.

Something about the soft word made my whole family stop and follow our gaze.

The town alarm rang out. The Dragon Watch had already spotted him. Doost's form was distant and yet far too close. He flew lazily around the town as if unconcerned. As if, possibly, even looking for me.

"Go," I hissed under my breath as my family frowned at the sky and pointed at him.

"Any moment now," my father reassured us.

It had the opposite effect on me.

The Dragon Watch was likely aiming as we spoke.

One arrow was all it took. *Why hadn't he listened to me?*

Doost circled in predictable patterns.

I couldn't breathe.

He banked toward the other side of the town as if he spotted me, just as the flaming arrow shot out.

It missed him by a mere handbreadth.

He reacted in the worst possible way. Instead of fleeing, the arrow made him fly closer to get a better look.

I covered my mouth with both hands to hold in a cry as the worst happened.

The next arrow didn't miss.

22

Doost

A ROAR RIPPED OUT of me. Fire filled the air, pouring from my lungs.

The humans had shot me. Fury surged. Instincts roared.

KILL THEM.

Only the pain stopped me, brought me back to myself, as it shot sparks of agony across my wing, making it impossible to level out.

Flapping my uninjured wing, I pushed to put some distance between myself and the town, but I couldn't slow my descent.

My animal instincts took over.

FLEE.

The ground rose up to meet me.

I crashed through the trees, which ripped at my wing, making me roar.

PAIN.

I hit the ground and then there was nothing.

23

Nes

THOUGH A DRAGON'S ARMOR was impenetrable, their wings were not. As the softest spot on a dragon, they were their only vulnerability; the shooter's aim was true.

I felt Doost's roar to my core as he plummeted. He spun out, falling sideways in a too-fast descent.

He seemed to realize the severity of his mistake too late, using his claws to dig out the arrow in the midst of his free fall. Once he flung the shards of the metal arrow away, his fall slowed a bit, but flying was clearly painful and growing worse by the second.

He launched himself through the air away from town, getting lower and lower but thankfully gaining distance.

When his body crashed into the forest, it was too far to feel the shudder of his impact through the earth, but we watched the trees bend and snap beneath him, until all we could see was them swaying in the aftermath of his landing.

Tears sprung to my eyes and my hands flew to my mouth to cover the hitch of breath. This was all my fault.

"We'd best go into town," Baba said to Roohstam, not noticing my reaction. "Looks like we may be needed for a dragon hunt."

They took the carriage and left in a hurry as darkness fell. The lamps in the wagon cast shadows on their serious faces.

"Let me come with you," I begged, but Baba wouldn't hear it.

At first, I paced in the courtyard while my sisters and mother tried to reason with me. "They'll be fine," they said. "They'll be with dozens of other men. The dragon won't stand a chance."

That only made me more upset. If the hunters found Doost, I'd never forgive myself.

I paced back and forth in front of the main window, not taking my eyes off the sky for a second, willing Doost to fly again, to get away.

The darkness settled over us and it became difficult to see.

Still, I watched for a dark shadow to cross the moon. Nothing.

"What's wrong, my little dragon hunter?" my mother said, coming to stand by me at the window.

I didn't meet her eyes. Debating whether or not I should tell her the truth, I pinched my lips together.

"You've never been afraid of the dragons before," Shadi said from the other side, startling me. Zareen stood quietly behind her, brow wrinkled.

"I'm not scared," I retorted, before I could think better of it.

They stared at me, waiting.

I returned to pacing. "I know him," I whispered, so soft I almost couldn't hear it. Saying it out loud sounded insane. This was nothing like when Avizun survived a dragon; this was more like comparing a dragon to a kitten. I bit my lip and stopped to face them, saying it louder anyway. "I *know* him." All three of them squinted at me. "He's not a dragon, he's a Jinni. And he's been cursed. And this is all my fault, because he's the one who brought me home, and I need to do something—"

Shadi rubbed her eyes. "I must be dreaming. You're not making sense."

I crossed my arms. Of course they didn't believe me.

With one last glance out the window, I made my decision. "I don't expect you to understand, but I can't just sit here and wait. I need to help him."

"He brought you back home?" My mother repeated my words slowly.

"Yes."

"And he's not really a dragon," Shadi drawled, unconvinced.

Zareen frowned. "You're saying he's a Jinni like Joram?"

"He's like Joram," I agreed. Then thought of my father's experience and added, "Except far better. He would never hurt me."

My mother shocked me by reaching out and pulling me into a hug. Her grip was painful. "If you must go, go."

I pulled back to look in her eyes. "Truly?"

She scowled, looking like she wanted to change her mind, but nodded, turning away.

I wrapped my arms around her even though she protested, unable to hide her tears. "Thank you."

I ran to my rooms before she could change her mind, grabbing the dragon-skin vest from where I'd dropped it by the tub. For some reason, it felt important to wear it. To declare the side I'd chosen. To let Doost know it was me and not a hunter that approached him—*if* I could get to him first.

Reaching the main level once more, my mother stopped me, handing me my old climbing bag. "I packed *kushta* for his wounds." She gestured to her side, where the arrow had pierced Doost's wing.

I nodded my thanks, breathless.

She wrung her hands. Zareen and Shadi stood wide-eyed behind her.

"I'll be okay," I reassured them with an optimism I didn't feel. "I'll be back soon."

I left the house on silent feet, pulling on the dragon skin and the bag.

The stables were empty; Baba and Roohstam had taken our only horse.

Opening the gate, I turned toward town and ran. The town square was visible in the distance, over the rooftops, lit orange by flames as if filled with dozens of torches. I needed a horse, and I needed to leave before the hunters.

The square was even more crowded than it had been earlier, with men, women, and children screaming their outrage and cheering on the Dragon Watch, where they scavenged the towers for heavy crossbows equipped with spears.

Between two people, I glimpsed Avizun leading the pack. "We will hunt down this dragon who dared threaten our village and kill it before it comes back!"

The people cheered, raising torches and weapons in agreement. The square was so brightly lit, it felt like midday. "I need every available hand not watching over Heechi to join me!" Another cheer.

Someone spied me at the edge of the crowd, aiming for the horses. "The egg girl should lead the way!" they yelled, to more cheers of agreement.

Once this would've been my dream.

To be a leader, to be seen as important. I still wanted those things—but not like this.

"No!" I shouted over them, pushing my way to the pedestal to join Avizun, uninvited.

Surprise made the hecklers grow quiet, giving me an opening to be heard.

"The dragon is not a threat! He won't hurt anyone. Trust me."

"So now the little egg hunter has become a dragon expert?" Avizun mocked and the crowd jeered.

My cheeks warmed, but I held firm. "He—it's a long story." I couldn't tell them how he'd dragged me to his cave, held me captive. That would only fuel their hate. "He's not like the other dragons," I screamed over their responding taunts to anyone who would listen. "He would never hurt anyone—I swear on a Jinni's honor. Just leave him alone!"

"Get her off the stage!" people yelled, and I was both pulled and pushed from it back into the crowd of disgusted faces, shaking their heads at me. At the opposite side of the crowd, I spied my father and brother staring at me, pale and wide-eyed. The shame and embarrassment I'd brought upon my family undoing all the good I'd done.

The town blacksmith stared me down. "You've been in the cliffs too long, girl."

"Did your time in the clouds make you forget about your people?" the butcher snapped from the other side of the crowd.

"We knew you were crazy, but now you've proved it," someone else shouted, and those who heard it laughed. Hands dragged me away, pushing me out of their midst, until I stood at the edge of the crowd.

Their opinion of me had changed again within mere minutes, as fickle as the weather.

"He fell from the sky near Srosh," Avizun shouted over their furious yells. "We leave the moment the harpoons are ready. Gather your supplies and meet at the edge of town."

"Why won't anyone believe me?" I cried, desperate to help Doost. But a month ago, I wouldn't have listened either.

I had done this.

It was because of me that he'd come here in the first place.

"Oh, we believe you," Avizun replied from nearby with a smirk. "Just like I believe Meymun over on Dragon Watch is really the prince of Jinn."

I took a deep breath. There was nothing else to be done, I had to say it. "The *dragon* is the prince of Jinn!"

A beat of silence was followed by an uproar of laughter. "Your father shouldn't let you out of the house," someone nearby said.

When hands reached for me again, I didn't give them a chance to grab hold. Pushing away, I ran down the streets until I reached the road where my father had left the horse and carriage.

My dragon-skin vest spooked the horse and I wasted valuable time calming him before he allowed me to untie him and place the spare saddle on his back, cinching it tight.

Roohstam and his friends were heading in my direction, all holding torches and laughing at his description of what he would do to the dragon when he found it.

I stepped into the stirrup and swung my foot over.

"What—? Nes, wait!" he yelled. "Stop! Father will—"

I didn't hear the rest.

I kicked the horse hard, and he burst into a gallop, taking off down the dark streets at a reckless speed. I glanced behind to make sure no one followed, thankful at least that I could lose them in the dark.

Angry fists shook in my wake, but no one took chase. The mob was convinced they knew where Doost would be, but I knew better.

Instead of heading east like they planned, I drove the horse toward the Dragon Cliffs in the north. The road in front of me blurred as the memory came back, before we'd left. Walking through the forest only hours ago, I'd reminded him yet again of our plan. *I'll meet you at the base of the Dragon Cliffs. Right below where we first met.*

It wasn't a lot to go on, but I had to hope. They probably expected him to stay put and lick his wounds. And they were right that he couldn't fly with an injury like that.

But he could walk.

And I had to believe I knew where he would go.

On foot, my journey would take a full day, but on horseback I crossed it in a fraction of that time, reaching the cliffs around midnight. The moon was at its peak in the sky.

The jeering of the townspeople had fallen silent. No doubt they'd left the safety of the town and now hunted soundlessly. Perhaps they'd even reached the spot where Doost had fallen. They were probably tracking him here even now. I was about to find out if I'd been right about him trying to reach our meeting place or not.

I tied my horse under the trees. He was skittish, most likely from the heavy dragon scent in the air by the cliffs. I sincerely hoped they wouldn't leave their resting places for a few hours more.

I ran across the open space between the trees and the cliffs until I could see down the length of them to the right and the left. Squinting in the light of the moon, I searched for any sign of him, but there was none.

Finding my old Jinni-rope where I'd left it almost a month ago, I tested its strength. Though a bit weathered and bleached by the sun, the Jinni magic had kept it strong and durable.

I began to climb.

Thankfully the moon was bright enough to reveal handholds. I was desperately out of shape. My arms quickly began to tremble.

Once above the trees, I stopped to survey the nearby area. *Will I be able to spot his shape moving through the trees?* I bit my lip, unsure.

Scanning the forest that stretched before me, I searched the dark woods for the place he'd fell. Or at least, somewhere within the vicinity. Just past it was the road where the townspeople would be fast approaching.

"Please be as tough as you look," I muttered under my breath. "Otherwise I came all this way for nothing." My anxious tone belied my words. I didn't know what I'd do if I'd been wrong and they were attacking him at this very moment. I should've protested harder. Should've found a way to make them see.

Seated on a small ledge of the cliff wall, I studied the forest, unblinking, searching for movement.

Nothing.

An hour passed, and another, and another.

It had to be getting close to dawn.

My lip was raw from chewing on it.

Still, I kept watch.

Something caught my eye in the dark. A shift of leaves. Branches leaning farther than seemed natural in the wind. A glint of moonlight on scales, headed toward me.

It stopped.

Without thinking, I flung myself out onto the rope and belayed down with reckless abandon.

As soon as my feet touched the ground I flung the ropes away and ran, never taking my eyes off the spot where I'd last seen movement.

"Where did you go?" I gasped as I ran. I tripped over roots, invisible under the trees where the moonlight didn't reach. After a nasty fall left me with a sharp pain in my knee and the sticky, wet warmth of blood trickling down my leg, I slowed a bit.

Dawn was beginning to break, but it was still dim beneath the canopy of trees, a dark gray that made everything blend together.

The forest was oddly still.

No sign of him.

Maybe he was farther back than I'd thought. Or maybe it hadn't been him at all; it could've been a bear or some other large creature.

I shook my head and kept going.

The first hints of sunlight peeked through the trees that grew denser, until it was a struggle to push through the undergrowth. I worried that I might be walking right past him. I didn't know which name to call out to him, but it didn't matter—I couldn't risk it. The dragons would wake soon, if not already, and their hearing was almost as strong as their eyesight. Any noise from me now would be asking to be eaten alive. So, I stayed silent and pushed on.

There, ahead. A dark black mound stood out behind the foliage. Shoving through the branches, I headed directly toward it, hoping against hope that he was still alive. His back was to me. And he wasn't moving. A lifetime of instincts kept me silent until I could confirm it was him and not some other dragon lying in wait.

His soft ears flicked at my approach, but otherwise he didn't move. That was a bad sign. As soon as I saw his yellow eyes open, I knew it was him.

They blinked and fell shut as I stepped closer.

"I'm so sorry," I whispered as I slowed to a stop in front of him, dropping to my knees by his head. Gently, I touched the warm scales on his snout, stroking his cheek. A drop of water fell on him and I realized I was crying. "This is all my fault. If you hadn't taken me home… I'm so sorry." I repeated it over and over, shaking my head as my vision blurred.

He groaned and his eyes stayed shut.

Hands clapped over my mouth, gripping my arm and ripping me away from the dragon.

I fought, kicking and throwing my elbows into whoever had grabbed me.

A soft *oomph* was all they allowed before more hands came to help and held me fast.

Furious, I struggled harder, until my eyes landed on Avizun across the small clearing.

He held a finger to his lips. As if I needed reminding of the dragons waking above.

With a wicked grin, he prepared his largest crossbow with a heavy spear. This was his favorite moment—the final shot that would take down his quarry.

Doost groaned again, unable to move.

Avizun must have been watching us. He'd known Doost wouldn't fly away. That's why he was taking his time. Savoring it.

The straps would be in place for his shot within seconds. I couldn't remember the last time I'd felt this helpless. Doost was going to die and it was all my fault.

His eyes snapped open, as if he'd heard me. With effort he lifted his head.

The hunters stepped back instinctively and Avizun fumbled with the extra weight of the spear on the crossbow.

I took advantage of their distraction and bit down on the hand covering my mouth. Hard.

With a hiss, the hunter let go.

An elbow to his stomach, followed by a heavy stomp on his instep, and his hands fell away completely as he curled inward.

The second hunter's hand tightened on my other arm, but I leaned into him instead, surprising him with a swift kick to the groin.

Both held in their groans admirably as they fell to the dirt.

Avizun looked up as I ran toward his weapon and he immediately lurched forward to grab me.

"Come any closer and I'll scream," I hissed, baring my teeth.

"You wouldn't dare," he growled back.

But he stopped.

Angling around until I stood between the weapon and Doost, I only said, "Try me."

Avizun's hands clenched and opened, spasming as he glared at me. "What's your plan, girl? You want to take the dragon down first, is that it? Be known as the greatest dragon hunter?"

"I don't care about any of that." The words surprised me by ringing true. "This isn't about reputation."

"Oh, no?" He glanced down at his nails, picking at the dirt beneath them. "Is that why you disappeared for a month and came back with a dragon's egg? So you could appear *humble*?"

He took a step forward, testing me.

"I said, *don't move*," I snapped, louder than I should, if only to remind him of my threat. "This is not a dragon. He's a Jinni under a curse—"

"Ahh yes, I've heard Maadar Bozorgi's stories," Avizun interrupted me, eyes glinting in the sunlight. He stood on his toes, prepared to pounce. He wouldn't let me stand here much longer. "We're all descended from dragons and all that nonsense."

"No—" I opened my mouth to argue that he had the story backward, that she claimed dragons descended from *our people.* But why was I arguing if I didn't believe it myself?

Somehow he'd gotten closer.

What if Maadar Bozorgi was right, though? After all, the land of Jinn had turned out to be far more real than I'd ever dreamed.

I stepped backward until I stood beside Doost's head. Too close to his sharp teeth and claws for Avizun to risk grabbing me.

His brows rose at my audacity, but he still glanced at his weapon, and I knew my nearness wouldn't stop him much longer.

"Listen, I know this is a long shot," I whispered so softly only Doost could hear me, "but I have to try." I reached out and placed my hand on the side of his head, stroking his long ear. I cleared my throat. "I think I might know your true name."

An awful fear spread throughout my limbs that I might be wrong. That I might be getting his hopes up for nothing, and on his deathbed at that. There was a good chance Maadar Bozorgi was wrong.

Too exhausted to growl or even keep his head up, he rested his chin against my knee and waited.

"I hope I'm doing this right," I mumbled, clearing my throat and placing my hands on his jaw once more. These could be his last moments. "Please try not to get killed, for me... *Malakai*."

2 4

Nes

HE REARED HIS HEAD back with a roar that echoed in the trees.

"Shh," I tried to hush him, panicking. I wasn't sure what to fear more, that the hunters would shoot him or that the dragons might heed his call. "Please! Stop!"

But he couldn't.

Agonizing roar after roar thundered through the valley. He thrashed wildly. I jumped just in time to avoid being hit by his tail, backing away in a rush. It knocked out the surrounding trees and Avizun's weapon, all in one great swing.

Avizun and the other hunters leapt back as well, and we could only watch the dragon uproot everything around him, crushing all vegetation and creating a flurry of dust and debris.

What have I done? Is the spell killing him?

There was nothing I could do to help.

The other hunters kept a safe distance, clearly judging the right moment to rush forward and attack.

The familiar tingle of Jinni magic stirred the air until the dust cloud grew so thick I lost sight of him.

His roars ended abruptly.

The hunters pressed back into the trees, fading out of sight as they whispered to each other not to waste arrows that might bounce off dragon scales, to wait for a visual.

I hesitated before dashing forward, entering the otherworldly wind.

"Malakai." I didn't know why I bothered to whisper after the racket he'd just caused. It felt odd to call him that. I'd grown so used to calling him Doost.

When I reached what I thought should be the center of the clearing he'd created, there was no sign of him. *What in all of Jinn just happened? He disappeared?*

As the dust settled bit by bit, it became clear there was no dragon here.

I spun around, searching the haze, confused, and nearly stepped on him.

There at my feet was a barefoot man wearing breeches and a torn shirt.

Or rather, a Jinni.

His black hair was long and tangled. He lay on his side, unmoving. I circled around to see his face. The bluish tint of his pale skin was the first thing I noticed, along with a long face, a strong jaw, and full lips. When his eyes flickered open, I almost expected them to be yellow and felt oddly unsettled to see they were the palest blue.

"Is it…? It can't be…" I whispered, swallowing hard at the attractive man before me. I didn't recognize anything of my friend in him.

As I squinted at him, he twitched the corner of his lip, the way Doost always had when he gave me a toothy grin, and I found myself slowly grinning back.

"I didn't really think it would work!" I laughed as I dropped to the ground in front of him, bracing my hands on the dirt as I leaned closer. "Are you hurt?" I reached out and touched his sleeve without thinking, distracted by the feeling of muscles underneath. I swallowed again and let go. My hand drifted to his side, where his wing used to be, but I didn't quite touch him again.

His voice came out low and uneven, and he coughed. "I'm well. Thanks to you."

My cheeks grew hot and I shook my head, confused. "But you were wounded…" I trailed off, not finding any trace of the injury.

As I sat back on my heels, perplexed, he lifted himself up on one elbow, pushing off the ground to sit up, testing. His muscles flexed underneath the fabric of a worn blue shirt that may have once been a rich, vibrant material.

"The arrow hit my wing." He shrugged, testing the new range of motion. A slow smile spread across those full lips that made me feel warm. "But I don't have wings anymore."

I stared at him, forgetting to respond as I took in his arms and legs. No more claws or scales or fangs either.

"I'm well. Jinni's honor, as you humans say," he said, standing, with another grin that I felt to my toes.

I lurched to my feet as well. When he took a step toward me, I unconsciously stepped back.

A frown wrinkled his pale forehead. "Nes." My name on his lips made my mouth dry. "You know me. It's only the outer form that's changed."

"I know, I know," I waved off his concern in embarrassment. "It's just, you look so different from Doost—ah, that is…"

"Malakai." He smiled.

"Malakai," I repeated, nodding like an idiot. I couldn't wrap my mind around his transformation. What an odd time to wish Shadi would've done my hair or that I would've let Zareen dress me. I licked my lips and tried to focus. "I can't believe…"

He glanced behind me.

I'd forgotten the hunters. Through the dust, they'd reappeared, weapons raised.

Avizun stood at the front of the group. "What trick is this?" he growled. "Where is the dragon?"

I stepped in front of Doost—*Malakai*—on instinct. "I told you. He's not a dragon. He was a Jinni under a curse."

Slowly, Avizun pulled the bolt of his crossbow back, setting the arrow into place for a shot. "Then turn him back into a dragon. And step aside."

Malakai tensed, lifting his hands to brush my arms, but I waved him away. "No. Go home. This hunt is over."

"It's over when I say it's over, girl," Avizun snapped, training the crossbow on us, taking aim.

I whirled at the soft whoosh of the arrow's release, pushing Malakai away.

His arms came around me; the world shifted in a flash.

We weren't impaled.

The hunters were gone, and we stood in another clearing, near the cliffs.

Whatever he'd done left me hunched over, gasping, as my stomach revolted. "What... just... happened?" I sucked in a deep breath until the ground stopped spinning.

My horse whickered from a short distance away. I jerked at the sound, startled to find we'd crossed the wide expanse of forest and returned to the cliffs in the span of a heartbeat.

"It's called traveling." He held out a hand to help me stand, but I waved him off, not trusting he wouldn't do it again, and straightened on my own.

"It's awful."

His blue eyes danced with amusement. I'd grown so used to reading him that I knew what he was thinking before he said a word.

"Yes." I crossed my arms defensively once more. "*Much* worse than flying. Or at least, a very close tie."

I glanced again at my horse, across the clearing where I'd left him. He hadn't been allowed to cool down after the frantic ride here, and he stomped his feet anxiously. The Dragon Cliffs stretched high behind us.

Malakai had carried us across a vast distance as if simply taking a step.

I let out a breath and looked him up and down, trying to wrap my mind around it all. He was taller than me. My eyes naturally landed on his lips, which quirked in a smile.

"What year is it?" he asked.

When I told him, some of the light left his eyes. "That's longer than I thought. I've been in dragon form for…" His voice dropped to a whisper. "At least a year now."

I didn't know what to say to that.

We stood in silence for a long minute.

It was a lot to take in.

As I stared up at him, he reached out to tuck my hair behind my ear. It felt strangely intimate, as did the way his voice grew deeper and lowered to a soft whisper when he pulled back. "I've always wanted to do that."

Somehow, that helped me find my voice. Shaking my head at him, intentionally loosening the hair, I forced a laugh. "Are all Jinn as forward as you, or are you especially flirtatious for your kind?"

"Neither." Instead of responding to my taunts, he grew serious. "Only with you."

"Mm-hmm." I ignored the butterflies in my stomach, turning to shade my eyes and search for any sign of the hunters. Or dragons. Though there were a few half-hearted roars as if responding to Doost, none appeared. Changing the subject, I glanced over at him. "I suppose you don't really need a ride anywhere, do you?"

He shook his head and his lips twitched, holding back a grin.

"Do you… need a place to stay?" I'd never asked a Jinni into my home before. I wondered if my mother would faint. Loosening my arms, I tried to relax. "My horse is just over there. We can ride to my home and I can hide you—" I cut off, having been about to say *in my bedroom,* but this was the *prince of Jinn.* I'd figure out some place. "It's the least we can do after everything you've done."

"The egg was helpful, then?"

I forced myself to meet his eyes as I answered. "Very. I can't thank you enough."

"I was happy to help." The way his lips curved in a slow smile was distracting.

"Depending on what I find in the next minute, I may be equally happy to take you up on your offer of a place to stay."

"The next—" I cut off as he vanished. "Sure, go ahead," I muttered with a wave of my hand. "Don't explain where you're going. I don't need to know."

I strode toward my horse, untying him and leading him toward a small stream to drink.

The minutes dragged by.

I wasn't sure where to look for him, so instead I watched the edges of the forest for the hunters, though they couldn't possibly guess where we'd gone.

When he reappeared beside me at the stream, I jumped and let out a small squeak.

His lips were pursed at whatever he'd found. "It's as she said, the portal to Jinn is completely invisible from this side. There's no going back that way."

She?

Ah. I remembered that day not so long ago. *The queen of Jinn.*

I cleared my throat. "The entire town of Heechi is out hunting you—in both your dragon form and your current form. It'd probably be best if you lie low for a few days."

At the way his eyebrow quirked, I answered his unspoken question the way I'd grown used to, before he even asked. "I'm not telling you what to do." I threw up my hands defensively. "I just don't know where else you could go. At least come to my family's home and get a hot meal and a night's rest before you go."

"That would mean a great deal to me, thank you."

I chewed on my lip. I couldn't believe what I was about to ask. "Does this 'traveling' work on horses as well?"

* * *

IT'D TAKEN SOME CONVINCING. Something about the unbreakable laws of Jinn, and how he didn't want to upset my family.

"There's no getting around that," I'd said, rolling my eyes. "They'll be upset no matter what you do. Your very presence will be upsetting. And they'll love every minute of it."

The corner of Malakai's mouth lifted and he shook his head. "I've always wanted to tell you how persuasive you are. So be it. Describe which home in that town was yours, and I can get us there unseen."

Soon we stood in smelly clothes before my mother, father, and siblings, as they all spoke at once.

The volume in the room was embarrassing. No doubt my face was a vivid shade of red.

I cleared my throat, turning to Malakai. "Would you excuse us a moment?"

He nodded, and vanished.

That shut them up.

"This is the *prince* of *Jinn*," I hissed, hoping Malakai couldn't hear from where he was. "Show some respect! And also, gratitude. It's because of him that we were able to pay our debts, and have money to spare."

My mother stiffened. "*He* is behind it? I refuse to take charity—"

Malakai appeared beside me, as if he'd never left, clearing his throat. "I do apologize," he said into the pocket of silence that his little trick always made. "I couldn't help overhearing. I may have helped a bit in regard to the egg, but your daughter made every bit of that coin on her own." He stood tall and confident, but shifted slightly, the only sign he might be nervous. "If my presence is an inconvenience, I would never want to intrude."

"Nonsense!" My father waved a magnanimous hand. "We welcome any man—er, Jinni—into our home who would aid our Nesrin."

My mother nodded, pacified by Malakai's pretty prose. "We'll make up a guest room for you. On the *other* side of the house," she added, in a poorly veiled warning to me.

I hadn't even told her I'd considered letting him into my bedroom. I crossed my arms and tried not to roll my eyes. As if doors would stop him if he wanted to visit me. My cheeks started to burn again. *Will he want to come visit me?*

* * *

I PACED IN MY bedroom. My mother had made it clear I was to leave the "poor prince" in peace to clean up for breakfast. Like a civilized lady.

I snorted. If Malakai thought me civilized after everything we'd been through, he'd be a fool.

My siblings had tried to get the story out of me, but I was too anxious to talk to anyone else until I'd talked to Malakai. I chased them off. My mother and father were no doubt working hard on making the house and the morning meal acceptable to a prince. For now, I was alone.

The sun seemed to be hinged in the sky. It had ceased to move completely. I would most likely starve to death and never have my questions answered.

Pacing the worn carpet in my bedroom from the door to the window, to the chair and then the bed, and back again, I jumped at a knock on the door. "It's me," a deep voice called through, adding, "Malakai."

I hurried to open the door, swinging it wide.

He stepped through.

Only as I closed the door and turned to face him did I see my bedroom through his eyes. Ragged bedcovers, patches on the pillows, faded paint and dusty furniture. For the first time in years, I agreed with my mother, and wished I'd cleaned up a bit more. I crossed my arms, feeling oddly shy.

Malakai turned to face me. His height surprised me again. Normally I was as tall as most men, but he looked down at me. "I wanted to thank you once more," his deep voice rumbled in his chest, somehow reminding me of his dragon form.

I found myself missing that form. I licked my lips and offered, "I'm so happy it worked. I honestly didn't know if it would."

His blue eyes darkened and he glanced away. "If I'm being truthful, I had little faith that it would. It was mostly instinct that made me take you in the beginning." His words came out in a rush. "Though I'm deeply grateful for how things have turned out, I wanted to offer my sincerest apologies for both scaring you and for tearing you away from your home against your will. If I'd been myself, I never would've allowed it."

"I know." My voice was barely louder than a whisper. That answer hardly seemed enough after his confession. I cleared my throat. "I'm glad you took me."

His eyes lifted from the floor to my eyes, studying me. "You offer a kindness I don't deserve," he said finally. "I know I'm running out of time. I'd lost hope, to be honest, that I'd stop the Crowning Ceremony."

Time. Crowning Ceremony. "The queen of Jinn said she'd bring you back after this Crowning Ceremony, right? So why do you want to stop it?"

He nodded. "Every fifty years, on the last day of summer, the reigning sovereign of Jinn must remove the Crown. This severs the enchantment. Otherwise the Crown will constantly enhance their Gifting, strengthen them, and afford them absolute control." He ran a hand through his hair, then paused to look at the ends of it in his hand, as if startled to see how long it'd gotten. "If my mother stands uncontested, she'll be crowned anew. But if an heir to the throne challenges her—if *I* challenge her—she must concede the throne, and the Crown, to me."

My brows rose. "Why?"

"That's how it's always been."

"So *this*—" I gestured to him with one hand, before crossing my arms once more—"this *curse* is her way of stopping you?" My voice lifted, incredulous. "How could she do that?"

He sighed, glancing around the room for a place to sit, as if too tired to stand any longer.

I waved him over to the chairs by the window, perching on the chair across from him, wishing there was more than a tiny thimble table between us, and at the same time wishing there was less.

"She's kept her crown for the last three Crowning Ceremonies. The Jinn have grown restless. I never wanted to force her out, but I spoke with her about this coming reign, about it being time for her to step down. And I had *thought* she'd listened."

"Why do you want her to step down?" I whispered, wide-eyed.

"Believe it or not, the humans and the Jinn used to be on friendly terms," he said softly. His eyes lingered on my face. "There didn't used to be this tension. The unbreakable laws of Jinn—"

The laws he'd explained to me earlier, that I'd already forgotten.

He caught my frown—he paid far too close attention—and reminded me, "Gifts are not allowed to be used for deceit, stealing, or to harm another."

"Ah, yes." I nodded, though I wasn't entirely sure where he was going with this.

"These unbreakable laws are being broken." His fists clenched on the table between us, and he leaned forward. "With more and more frequency, I'm afraid. Not only here in human lands, but in Jinn itself under the queen's own hand."

I swallowed, but didn't reply. I didn't know what to say to that.

"She wants to rule another fifty years, with the power of the Crown, and all its spells that keep her young and make her magic stronger than any other in all of Jinn. No one can match her. No one can stop her. Except for an heir, during the Crowning Ceremony, when she is forced to relinquish the Crown, however briefly."

"To you," I confirmed.

He nodded.

Somehow I needed to hear it twice. "You're the only one who can stop her."

"I am." He fell silent, frowning.

At first, I thought I'd upset him. So much of him was a mystery to me and I'd never realized it before—it was like sitting next to a friend and a stranger, all at the same time.

Glancing over at him in the awkward silence, I studied his profile. He was shockingly handsome. And so serious.

He glanced over at me, and my cheeks warmed, even though he didn't know what I'd thought.

"It's my duty to stop her," he said after a long pause.

I tried to gather my thoughts, which had abandoned me. The reminder of where he was from made my entire body feel leaden and stiff. I'd forgotten I was in the presence of royalty.

Malakai wasn't just any Jinni.

He was the prince.

The vivid memory of his meeting with the queen returned to me.

The way she'd placed her hand on his cheek.

Called him darling.

"Just to be clear... the one who did this to you, the queen of Jinn," I breathed, staring at him. "She's your own mother."

The way his face twisted in pain before he spoke confirmed it. "Yes."

"How could a mother do such a thing?"

"Sometimes family doesn't love you the way you need," he said softly. "Sometimes they love something else more."

"I'm so sorry." I wanted to touch him somehow in comfort, but I couldn't bring myself to move.

"That's not the worst of it." The prince of Jinn stared down into my eyes and I forgot to breathe. "I still have to stop her."

Epilogue

Malakai

COULD I TRUST HER?
I wanted to.

THE END.

***

Will Malakai fall for Nesrin? Want to know how their story collides with Arie, Kadin, Rena, Gideon, and Bosh? Read the epic finale, The Enchanted Crown, to find out!

Arie, Rena, and Nesrin come together in the fourth book of The Stolen

Kingdom Series...

**TURN THE PAGE FOR A SNEAK PEEK AT THE
ENCHANTED CROWN**

"HAS ANYONE SEEN THE queen?" Kadin's warm, deep voice floated through the library door from out in the hall, tense and clipped.

The servant's response was inaudible.

I strained to hear their thoughts but was met with silence—a painful reminder of what I'd lost when my Gift was Severed a couple months ago.

Muffled footsteps grew louder, heading my way.

I'd found a dark pocket of space beneath the library stairs, which the sunlight didn't know existed, and neither did anyone else.

There was an old rolled-up rug, left forgotten in the tiny space, which I used as a cushion to sit on. I leaned back and stared out at the small triangle of light in front of me. It revealed the last few shelves of a dusty bookcase in the corner, as well as the legs of a single chair and table. The main library door and the rest of the room were out of sight, which meant I was too.

Still, I pressed farther back into the darkness, tucking my slippered feet beneath the heavy skirts of my black mourning dress. Mourning the loss of my father. Of my Gift. Of my entire life as it had once been.

Leaning my head against the wall, my fingers idly traced the patterns of the cracks. There was a chip in the paint. I picked at it.

"Arie?" Kadin called, inside the large room now, breaking library etiquette to raise his voice. "Are you here?"

Reluctantly, I pulled my gaze from the wall.

His boots strode past my hiding place as he took the stairs to the second level.

"If you're here, you're needed in the dungeons." He raised his voice to reach the entire library, which I assumed was empty, though I hadn't checked thoroughly before crawling under the stairs.

His steps overhead grew louder, then quieter, then louder again as he paced down one row of books after another, likely hoping I'd materialize behind one of them.

It should've bothered me that he assumed I was ignoring him.

Instead, tears welled up as I noticed the empty space where his thoughts should've been.

I heard nothing.

Only a chair squeaking across the floor as he moved it in his search.

I sank back against the wall and closed my eyes.

My Severance had been incredibly effective. It'd cut me off from my abilities and myself in ways I'd never imagined.

Gideon had told me once that a Severance was like losing a limb or a lung, that a Gift was a part of you.

I'd scoffed at the idea then.

But the loss was *more* than both of those things combined. My whole body tingled, and my hands twitched restlessly, as if searching for something that wasn't there. The absence of my ability carved out something inside of me, leaving me hollow and too light, floating along through each day without an anchor to hold me to reality.

Kadin was still calling out, although softly, as if worried the wrong ears might overhear. His voice grew closer as he came back down to the main level. "The people need their queen, Arie. Please. We need you." His voice hitched just a bit but came back clear and strong. Maybe I'd imagined it. "There's… someone you need to see."

Someone.

In the dungeons.

Kadin's effort to be discreet was a waste of time. The servants already knew the guards had caught a spy this morning. I'd overheard them whispering about it earlier when I'd hidden behind a tapestry. *Is he from King Amir's kingdom or another's?* they'd asked each other. *Is there a war brewing while the kingdom of Hodafez is left defenseless?*

I played with a little purple thread I'd pulled from the carpet, wrapping it around my finger, then unwrapping, then wrapping again.

I should care.

It should've bothered me that I didn't.

Kadin's sigh pulled me out of my dark thoughts. Leaning forward on my hands and knees, I snuck a glance at him from the depths of my hidden alcove.

There were dark circles smudged blue and purple under his golden-brown eyes. His dark hair had grown past his ears, and his beard had begun to fill in. A muscle in his jaw twitched as he gazed around the room one last time, frowning.

"Have you found her?" It was Gideon's voice, somewhere just out of sight.

How long has he been there? Normally I'd have sensed him immediately—that tingle of another Gifting present. Not anymore. Whenever I poked at the place my Gift had been, it was like poking at a hole in the gums where a tooth had been: surprise and confusion followed swiftly by loss, and sensitive to the touch.

Kadin only shook his head, lips pursed.

I crawled backward to the rug again. Carefully, to avoid being heard, I unrolled it to lie down, lifting my heavy crown from my head and placing it at my feet so I wouldn't have to look at it.

"I could move forward without her, but I would prefer her permission." Gideon's soft voice washed over me like a distant wave.

I tried to tune him out.

"The queen of Jinn uses human spies as well," he added. "We may need to consider that possibility." They moved toward the door and back into my line of vision. "Enoch hasn't returned since he left to spy on the queen, so I can only assume they've found him and that he's been imprisoned… or worse."

"Do you trust him now?" Kadin asked. His back was to me. From the stiff way he stood, I guessed he didn't.

"I do," Gideon replied, eyes dropping to the floor. "He was controlled by the queen's amulet, just as I was."

"I notice you give him grace but blame yourself." Leave it to Kadin to say what Gideon and I had danced around for months. We'd avoided each other's presence. I knew my Severance wasn't his fault.

It wasn't.

Repeating it had yet to change the memory of a bitter iron taste on my tongue from biting it, or the twisting fear that spiraled up inside me in his presence.

"You speak the truth," Gideon whispered in his way of an answer without answering anything. His usually sharp blue eyes still gazed aimlessly at the floor.

"If King Amir had forced Enoch to do the Severance instead of you, as he'd originally intended, would you have held him accountable?"

"No." Gideon's voice was flat.

"It was the king's vendetta," Kadin insisted. "You were only a tool."

"A tool would not feel responsible." Gideon's expression flickered, and he straightened. "It's neither here nor there. My focus now must be on not making the difficulties worse. To ease her burden however I can. Which means this situation must be taken care of."

Kadin nodded, rubbing a hand across his face. Turning away from Gideon, he stared toward my section of the library.

I held my breath and didn't move.

When he didn't think anyone was looking, his expression grew hopeless. Where his lips normally quirked upward with a spark of mischief and adventure, they now flattened in a grim line.

Gideon continued. "While Queen Jezebel won't declare outright war on the human world until after the Crowning Ceremony, I can only guess at what she's doing behind the scenes."

Kadin's shoulders rose and fell in a heavy breath, and his eyes roamed the shelves in front of him aimlessly, crossing over my hiding spot once more. His expression didn't change. He turned to face Gideon. "It's been this way for three months now. If you want to act in Arie's best interest, I'd recommend not waiting for her when you know what you need to do."

I frowned at his back. Had it really been three months since the Severance? It felt as if it'd just happened yesterday, and at the same time as if it'd taken place years ago.

Rolling over to face the wall, I curled my legs inward and wrapped my arms around myself, closing my eyes. Two sets of footsteps made their way out of the library, and the door shut behind them.

The silence wrapped around me like a thick shell that kept everything else out. Some small part of me, as insubstantial as a shadow, whispered that I should follow, while another larger part wished they would leave me alone permanently. I wasn't who they thought I was. I couldn't be what they needed. It was better for everyone this way. The shadow side agreed.

But another small voice wished someone would find me…

A soft scuff of a footstep sounded.

My eyes flew open, and I spun around to find the object of my thoughts crouching in the little triangular opening. He'd seen me after all.

"Is there room on this rug for two?" Kadin asked softly.

I dipped my chin in a nod, averting my eyes.

He tucked himself inside the small space beside me, our knees knocking together.

I rolled onto my back to make room.

I didn't want his pity.

What I hadn't expected was his arm gently wrapping around my waist and arm. Holding me. His warmth seeped into me, making me aware of my icy skin. My arms drew up to cover his instinctually.

The minutes passed as we lay there without speaking, and his breathing evened out until he began to snore softly. This gave me the courage to glance over at his face, so close to mine. The worry lines relaxed in sleep, and his lips parted slightly.

I stared at the low ceiling above us as tears threatened to escape. One trickled down my cheek into my ear.

The shell was still there, but this time I wasn't alone inside it.

ORDER BOOK FOUR IN THE SERIES!
BOOKS2READ.COM/THEENCHANTEDCROWN

THANK YOU FOR READING!

If you loved this book, support the author by
***leaving a review**—it helps more than you know!*

ALSO BY
BETHANY ATAZADEH

THE STOLEN KINGDOM SERIES :

THE STOLEN KINGDOM

THE JINNI KEY

THE CURSED HUNTER

THE ENCHANTED CROWN

THE COLLECTOR'S EDITION

THE QUEEN'S RISE SERIES :

THE SECRET GIFT

THE SECRET SHADOW

THE SECRET CURSE

THE NUMBER SERIES :

EVALENE'S NUMBER

PEARL'S NUMBER

MARKETING FOR AUTHORS SERIES :

HOW YOUR BOOK SELLS ITSELF

GROW YOUR AUTHOR PLATFORM

BOOK SALES THAT MULTIPLY

SECRETS TO SELLING BOOKS ON SOCIAL MEDIA

PLAN A PROFITABLE BOOK LAUNCH

GLOSSARY

Ahmadi (Ah-MAH-dee) – Nesrin's family surname

Amir (Ah-meer) – the King of Sagh

Avizun (Ah-VEE-sun) –the best hunter who's found the most egg pieces

Baba – persian word for father

Bache (Bah-chay) – persian word for children

Barnabas (Bar-nah-bus) – the Jinni turned into a wolf

Daleth – a Jinni portal into the human world (the Hebrew word for door)

Dokhtari (Dukt-tar-ee) – a title of affection (persian word for daughter)

Doost (Dew-st) – name given to the dragon (persian word for friend)

Heechi (Hee-chee) – town where Nesrin lives (persian word for nothing)

Jezebel (JEZ-zuh-bell) – queen of the Jinn

Jinn/Jinni (Gin/GIN-nee) – Jinn is the name of the country and the race
   of Jinn as a whole (i.e. *the Jinn, the land of Jinn*); Jinni is the singular,
   used to refer to an individual Jinni and also as a possessive (i.e. *a
   Jinni, a Jinni's Gift*)

Joram (Jor-rum) – a Jinni hired by Nesrin's father to help him

Khaanevaade (Hah-nah-vah-DAY) –a fable even older than the Jinn, the
   supposed ancestors of dragons (persian word for family)

Kushta – an herb that helps healing occur faster and soothes the body,
   works differently depending on the form it's in

Maadar (Moh-DAR) – persian word for mother

Maadar Bozorgi (Moh-DAR Boh-ZOORG-ee) – an old woman in
   Heechi who most people think is crazy (persian word for
   grandmother)

Malakai (MAL-uh-kye) – what Maadar Bozorgi thinks is the name of
   the prince of Jinn

Meymun (May-MOON) – side character mentioned (persian word for
   monkey)

Roohstam (Roost-tom) – Nesrin's older brother

Sagh (Saw-gh) – a human kingdom, ruled by King Amir (persian word for dog)

Shadi (Shah-dee) – Nesrin's older sister

Shah – interchangeable title for a governer of provinces within a kingdom or for a monarch (persian word for king)

Shah's Council – a council of local Shahs from across the kingdoms that meets to decide common laws and rules

Srosh – city near Heechi

Zareen – Nesrin's youngest sister

Three Unbreakable Laws of Jinn:

1) Never use a Gift to deceive
2) Never use a Gift to steal
3) Never use a Gift to harm another

Bethany Atazadeh is best known for her young adult fantasy novels, The Stolen Kingdom series, which won the Best YA Author 2020 Minnesota Author Project award. She is a mama to a cute little boy and a corgi pup, and is obsessed with stories and chocolate.

Using her degree in English with a creative writing emphasis, Bethany enjoys helping other writers through her YouTube aka "AuthorTube" writing channel and Patreon page.

If you want to know more about when Bethany's next book will come out, visit her website below where you can sign up to receive monthly emails with exciting news, updates, and book releases.

CONNECT WITH BETHANY:
Website: www.bethanyatazadeh.com
Instagram: @authorbethanyatazadeh
YouTube: www.youtube.com/bethanyatazadeh
Patreon: www.patreon.com/bethanyatazadeh

ACKNOWLEDGMENTS

Huge thank you to you, my reader, for being a fan of this series. It means so much to me.

I have the best team surrounding me, no question about it. I'm so thankful for each person who has helped me craft this story and grow as a writer.

My critique partners, Brittany Wang and Jessi Elliott, who read messy rough drafts and helped me find the useable elements, and equally important, caught the stuff that didn't belong. Their feedback takes my writing to the next level.

To my beta readers, Amelia Nichele, Athena Marie, Bri R. Leclerc, Elizabeth Hamm, Emma Woodham, Katherine Schober, Kyra Hunter, and Lia Anderson, you are all amazing. I loved reading your notes on the things you enjoyed, as well as the things that were confusing. Your feedback shaped the direction of this book. It's because of YOU that there is a second point of view besides Nesrin's, and it makes the story so much more exciting!

This was my first time working with my amazing editor, Natalia Leigh, and I was blown away by her professionalism as well as by her detailed feedback.

I also want to shout out my amazing cover designer, Mandi Lynn (Stone Ridge Books), who let me word vomit all my ideas and then somehow managed to pull them together into this gorgeous piece of art on the cover.

Finally, to my amazing patrons who support me over on Patreon, I wanted to shout out each of you who supported me during my release month, June 2020, as a thank you:

thank you to my patrons:

365daysofbipolar, Aaron Dumas, Abbie Mattson, Adam Beswick, Agnes Anne, Alicia Ariail, Alx LeFrey, Alyssa Green, Amanda Creek, Angel Guice, Anna Zappia, Annie, Antonio M. Smith, April McCall, Ashleigh Hage, Ashley, Ashley Price, Ashley Shiflett, Athena Marie, Author Brittany Wang, Avery Huxley, Bailey Damron, Bethalison20, Bhavana Maitri, Bill Atkinson, Brandi Sumey, Bri Leclerc, Caffeine and Composition, Cam Meze, Carla Calvert, Caroline Southwell, Caylie Mosset, Claerie Kavanaugh, Courtney Corboy, Cynthia Carbonneau, Danielle Hippman, David Stamper, Debra Sennefelder, Desiree Philmore, DjanB, Dominique Mitchell, Donna Marie Tyree, Dot, Elijah Parks, Elissa Kane, Elizabeth Amos, Elizabeth Duivenvoorde, Emily Hallblade, Emma Woodham, Erik Zidowecki, Erika, Esther Diaaz, Falan Rowe, Fiachraface, Francesca Wilson, Gabriella Slade, Greta, Hailey Bridges, Hannah McMillin, Hayley, Heather, Heather Venkat, Holly Davis, Ingrid, J S Roberts, Jack Silver, Jade Yap, Janet Y. Perkins, Jasmine, Jen Kropf, Jen Morris, Jenai Logan, Jennifer Winni White, Jessica Renwick, JJ Otis, Jodie Duxbury, Joe Musulin, John Charles Wilson, John Jeng, Julia Stilchen, Kassie Dunn, Katherine Dix, Kathryn Marie, Katie Cavinder, Katy, Kayla, Kayla Eshbaugh, Kaylee White, Kellilynne Johnson, Kenneth Lybech, Kent Lofgren, Kenya Dawkins, Keri Wyllie, Kirsten Hicks, Kristina Allardice, Kristy Walker, Kyra Hunter, Lacy Hess, Leilani Lopez, Lesley Barklay, Leslie Arambula, Lisa Farver, Lisa Vance, Lisandra Tejada, Literatura Por Correio, malin Victoria Søvik, Mandi Lynn, Margarita Lapina, Martin Marquez, Mary Long, Mary Wockenfuss, May Bhank, meagan macarthur, Melanie Clark, Michelle C., Michelle Cantwell, Michelle Patrick, Mie96, Natalie Roberts, Neta, Nikkita Bell, Orla Byrne, Orn Einarsson, Ose, QueenBritters, Randy Bishop, Rebecca, Rebecca Armstrong, Rebecca K. Sampson, Rhiannee Williams, Rob Rostau, Rosa Snapp, Rosanne Bowman, Rox Alvarado, Ryn Willis, Samantha Traunfeld, San Diego Gary, Scribbling Kat, Sharon Muha, Shauna Skelton, Shirsten Shirts, Sierra Rice, Sofia Osório, Sondae Stevens, Stephanie, Stephanie Derbas, Stephanie Durocher, Stephanie Van den Bos, Susan Watson, Sydney, Sydney Rain, Tehlissa Hillsmon, Temecka Evans, Teneasha Pierson, Terri Spero, Timi Lee, Timothy Miller, TJ Carr, Valerie Johnson, Vanessa Michelle Roberson, Veronica Agostini, Veronica Arnesen, Victoria Ellis, Vivien Reis, Wendy Rogers, Will Rivett, Zoe

Printed by BoD™in Norderstedt, Germany